COMBUSTIBLE

A SAM LAWSON MYSTERY

DAVID K WILSON

1

He didn't notice her at first.

Joe Reddington shut the door behind him and tossed the motel room key on the cheap dresser. The small window air conditioner rattled loudly as it futilely attempted to fight the East Texas heat. Joe noticed the bedspread and sheets had been pulled off of the full-size bed. The bedspread lay in a heap on the dingy dark blue carpet.

He checked his watch. 3:04 p.m. He had told her to meet him at 3:00.

As he started to unbutton the shirt of his guard uniform, he noticed a light coming from the partially shut bathroom door.

"Maria!" he barked. "I don't have much time."

He sat on the edge of the bed to take off his brown work boots, the mattress groaning loudly under his massive frame.

That's when he saw her.

Through the crack of the bathroom door he could see her facing him. But something wasn't right.

"Maria?" he said quietly as he stood. "What are you doing?"

As he stepped toward the bathroom door, he realized what

was wrong. Her feet weren't touching the floor. Her body was dangling about six inches off the ground.

He swung open the door to find Maria's lifeless body hanging. One end of a sheet had been secured around an exposed support beam on the celling, the other end wrapped around her neck.

Joe stumbled backward in shock, he struggled to breathe. What had she done? His eyes were locked on Maria, hanging lifelessly in her maid's uniform.

He began to feel nauseous. Waves of emotion rolled over him. Disbelief. Fear. Confusion. "Why would she do this?"

Then he began to panic. What should he do now? Should he get her body down? Call the police? Get the hell out of there and leave her for someone else to discover?

In the barrage of dizzying thoughts, he reached for his cell phone and dialed a number.

As he listened to the phone ring, he looked at Maria's limp body hanging in front of him and the panic began to boil up into anger. She had screwed him over big time.

2

Six months later...

The smoke hit his lungs hard, but Sam Lawson fought back the urge to cough as he walked inside the two-story home. He didn't want the other cops to think a little smoke bothered him. Square-jawed and just over six feet tall, Sam was a handsome man with a formidable presence. But age and hard living were beginning to take their toll on the forty-year-old detective, and he had to work a little harder to make an impression on the younger cops.

Two of those younger cops met Sam at the base of the staircase. Officer Jim Telford, the taller of the two, grinned.

"Hey, Sam," he said with a nod.

"Jimbo!" Sam replied a little too loudly. "How's it hanging?"

Sam noticed the other officer, Mike Neely, shaking his head in disapproval. "I'm sorry, Mike. How rude of me. Is yours hanging okay, too?"

Officer Neely rolled his eyes and walked away. Sam and

Officer Telford moved to the side to let two firefighters pass them.

"What happened to you?" asked Telford, pointing at Sam's swollen nose.

Sam had almost forgotten about the fight. Although, technically, it was less of a fight and more like a beast of a man using Sam as a private punching bag in a public bar. His attacker was an ex-con who still harbored a grudge against Sam for arresting him a year earlier. Luckily, he only landed a couple of punches before Sam was able to buy his way out of further abuse. Sam had been around enough drunks to know they liked one thing more than fighting: free drinks.

He had just given the bartender his last twenty when he got the call from Chief Kaster about an accidental death in a house fire. Sam's immediate reaction was to complain to the chief that he was off duty. Kaster didn't seem to care. The department was short-staffed and no one else was available. Besides, the chief assured him, it would require no more than a check-in. A man fell asleep smoking in bed. Nothing really to investigate.

When Kaster had asked if he had been drinking, Sam lied. Force of habit. Even though he was officially off duty, he knew Kaster already disliked him and Sam didn't want to give him any more ammunition. Getting called into work was probably for the best, anyway. Sam had been able to talk himself out of a solid beating once, but he was sure to eventually make a wisecrack that would break the peace. He couldn't help himself. Getting called away probably saved him a trip to the ER.

"Keeping the peace can get dirty sometimes, Jimbo." Sam said, finally answering the cop's question.

"Well, you should have at least popped a breath mint," Telford whispered. "You smell like a liquor store."

Sam cupped his hand over his mouth and breathed into it.

"More like a brewery," Sam corrected him with a wink. "Where's ground zero?"

"Top of the stairs," Officer Telford answered, pointing up to the doorway.

Sam glanced up the stairs then turned his attention to the disaster surrounding him. The first floor was dripping wet from the fire hoses. Smoke damage stained the walls, and furniture had been shoved out of the way by the firefighters. The blaze had been contained to a couple of rooms upstairs, but the entire house suffered for it. To Sam's untrained eye, the place seemed destroyed.

Sam smiled at Telford one last time and walked past him. He noticed the looks of disapproval from Officer Neely and some of the other uniformed cops and he shot them a wink. He was used to it. Some people just liked to judge. In fact, that was the reason he'd transferred from Houston to the smaller, more manageable city of Quinton five years ago. Not that Quinton was small—with just over 25,000 people, it was anything but quaint. A former manufacturing hub, the town had seen better days. The state prison was the current main source of employment. But, in spite of the prison, or maybe because of it, there wasn't a lot of serious crime. It was the perfect place for Sam to quietly ride out his career. Unfortunately, he still had a knack for finding trouble, and it hadn't taken long for him to re-establish a bad reputation.

He knew he should clean up his act, but, at this point, why bother? Being a cop could steal your soul if you let it. He almost made that mistake once and he sure as hell wasn't going to make it again.

Sam stepped over a fire hose and walked carefully up the slick stairs. Still a bit wobbly from the punches to the head (and the beer), he held on to the banister and navigated his way slowly. As soon as he reached the upstairs bedroom, he stopped himself.

"Holy shit."

3

Two spotlights were clamped on either side of the door, illuminating wisps of smoke that still clung to the night air. The wall behind the bed—now a large messy rectangle of black ashes—was completely burned away, exposing the room to the crowd that had gathered outside on the street. The humid night air filled the room, smothering the warmth that rose from the debris.

What remained of the walls, furniture and floors was scorched black. Portions of the floor boards were marked off with tape to keep people from stepping on them.

"Someone's been grilling steak," Sam said loudly to announce his presence.

"That would be the deceased's body," answered Tim Neiman. "Show a little respect."

A tall, thin, studious man in his early forties, Tim was the county's fire investigator. He was squatting next to what appeared to be the remains of a body that lay in the middle of the bed's ashes. Sam crouched next to him.

"That him?"

Tim didn't answer. Instead, he used the end of a pen to

move a piece of burnt cloth from the skull. The body was so badly burned, it was hardly even recognizable as a human. In his twenty-five years on the force, even including the two decades in Houston, Sam had never seen a burned corpse before. He tried to ignore the unease in his stomach.

Out of habit, he found himself making another joke. "Yeah. He's dead alright."

Tim ignored him and Sam stood slowly to hide his dizziness.

"Smoking in bed?" Sam asked.

Tim nodded. "I can't believe people still do that."

Sam turned his attention to the burnt dresser. It was nothing more than a frame now. The slightest touch, or even just a rustling breeze, would disintegrate it. Globs of melting glass shards were stuck to the top of it—most likely all that was left from framed family pictures. He made a mental note to look through the rest of the house for other photographs.

"Just this one?" Sam asked.

"Just him. Luckily, the wife and son weren't home."

"Wife and son?" Sam noted. "Where are they?"

Tim sighed impatiently. "I'm trying to conduct an investigation here."

Sam chuckled. "Whoa, buddy. Lighten up. We're on the same team. Just trying to get caught up."

Tim shot him a very annoyed glance.

"Right now, the deceased is assumed to be Joseph Redding-ton," Tim said, as if reading a report. "This is his house, where he lived with his wife and teenage son. No other bodies were found so, apparently, they weren't here at the time. Some of your boys are trying to contact them now."

Sam nodded, suddenly realizing he should have already pulled his notepad from his jacket pocket. That would have been good information to write down. But he knew it wouldn't go over well if he retrieved the notepad now and asked Tim to repeat himself.

Tim stared down at the charred remains. "At least he died quickly. Cheap, flammable sheets went up like a torch."

Sam looked over the remains and through the exposed wall. He could see a handful of people still gathered out front by the fire trucks.

"Alright. If you don't need me here, I'm heading out."

Tim answered with a nod, and Sam let out a sigh of relief a little bit more loudly than he meant to.

He felt stupid leaving so quickly, but he didn't know what value he could add. The guy was dead, and according to the fire inspector, it was a smoking accident. Not much for him to do. And, if he was being completely honest, he would rather get out of the house before the wife and kid showed up. He wasn't sober enough to be giving anyone bad news right now.

He scanned the room one more time before leaving, blissfully unaware that he'd be returning to the house very soon.

4

Francine gripped the steering wheel with both hands as she navigated through the neighborhood streets. Even though she drove these roads every day, it still made her nervous driving at night.

"Sure you don't want any fries?" her son Mitch asked.

She and Mitch had picked up some drive-thru burgers on their way home, but Francine wouldn't loosen her grip on the wheel long enough to eat. Mitch, on the other hand, had already scarfed down two double cheeseburgers and a large order of fries. Not that she was surprised. After football practice, Mitch always ate like he had a hollow leg.

Francine glanced over at her son and shook her head no. She could feel her freshly cut hair bounce at her shoulder. It felt different. Lighter. She had always worn her hair long and parted down the middle, but earlier in the day, a very persuasive hair stylist had given her a new cut with a side part.

She looked at herself in the rear-view mirror. She still didn't recognize her new look but she liked it. It seemed to highlight her ordinary features and actually made her feel pretty for the first time in a long time. In her late thirties, with a slight build and average height, she had always been the kind of woman that could walk through a room completely unnoticed.

Her son, on the other hand, was hard to miss. Mitch wasn't tall, but he was solid. Muscular with broad shoulders, he looked every bit like the star linebacker he was. But it was his eyes that really stood out. Piercing ice blue, his gaze had an intensity that was both attractive and intimidating.

"I still can't believe you were going to walk home," Francine said.

Mitch shrugged. "I do it all the time. It's no big deal."

"You need to call to let me know when you do that."

"I told you. My phone was dead," Mitch replied.

"Then keep a charger."

Mitch picked up Francine's phone. "You're one to talk."

She glanced down quickly at the dead screen of her phone and groaned.

"I got busy. And your dad has the charger."

"I have an extra one at home you can have," he replied matter-of-factly.

Francine smiled and patted her son's left knee. He was always taking care of her.

She looked out the window at the familiar line of houses. It was a blue-collar neighborhood in a fairly rural city. No fancy manicured yards or overly large homes. Just single-floor ranches with an occasional modest two-story breaking the pattern. Weathered vinyl siding. Yards that needed mowing. Pick-up trucks in every driveway. Lots of Texas flags.

When they turned the next corner onto Tillerson Avenue, they both immediately sat forward, peering out the windshield. Even though they were still a couple of blocks from home, they could see the red and blue lights shining through the darkness.

"Are those fire trucks?" Mitch asked.

Francine squinted her eyes to see better. Then, as they got closer, she gasped.

"That's our house!"

5

The next morning, Sam's head was pounding as he trudged up the stairs of the police station. With every painful step, he felt closer to throwing up. Maybe it wasn't such a good idea to have had that extra drink after leaving the scene of the fire. Or maybe it was the five or six after that one. At least he had the sense to cab it home.

He only slept for a couple of hours. Then he forced himself up early, cabbed it back to his car, and drove to the station to catch up on the paperwork he should have done the night before.

Sam was relieved to find he was the first one to arrive in the investigative unit. That meant he could work in quiet. He flipped the light switch and squinted as the blue fluorescents flickered on with an antagonizing hum. He walked to his desk, sat down with a thud, and squealed his chair forward.

Burger wrappers and coffee-stained papers covered every inch of space between his outdated monitor and office phone— its coiled cord twisted into a clustered knot. Sam turned on the computer and waited for the machine to power up, sipping the lukewarm coffee he'd picked up at the convenience store.

He made an attempt to clean up some of the mess on his desk by collecting the scattered papers into a single pile, then tossing it all into the trash bin. He picked up the small framed photo that had been hidden under the heap. It was of a handsome man in his early twenties with a smile eerily similar to Sam's.

"How you doing, Champ?" Sam asked the photo. "How's the wife and kid?"

Sam felt a slight pang in his heart every time he looked at the picture of his son. He hadn't actually seen him in over ten years. In fact, he'd printed the picture from Nick's Facebook page. Thank God for Facebook. It was the only way he knew anything about his son. Or his grandkid.

Sam had married Nick's mother right out of high school. They were high school sweethearts convinced they were going to beat the odds and stay together. And, for a while, it looked like they were going to do it. Everything was going great. Sam worked his way up to detective and, soon after, Susan got pregnant with Nick.

But, as had happened to many cops before him, the job started to take its toll. Sam had always faced life with a quick wit and lighthearted attitude. But a never-ending barrage of gruesome crimes and a deluge of innocent victims and family of victims started to weigh on him. Sam started to withdraw. He found himself working late and weekends. Avoiding his family. Maybe it was an obsession with finding justice for those less fortunate. Or maybe it was guilt that he had life so good while others didn't. Either way, the job swallowed him up. Finally, tired of being a neglected wife and single parent, Susan packed it up for the West Coast and took their five-year-old son with her.

Time, distance and resentment slowly drove a bigger wedge between the two and Susan soon asked for a divorce. Sam had tried to reconcile with his son a few times, but Nick had no interest. Sam couldn't blame him. He'd been a shitty, absentee dad and deserved every ounce of scorn thrown at him.

Sam shook off the memory. He had gotten pretty good at shaking things off in the fifteen years since he lost his family. He had learned his lesson the hard way and had vowed never to take anything seriously again. It wasn't worth the price.

It took Sam about a half hour to fill out the report on the fire. Luckily, he'd remembered to ask one of the uniformed cops for the victim's name and had faked his way through the rest. Just paperwork for an insurance claim, he thought to himself.

He looked up when he heard another detective walk in the office. Frank Bannon was a portly, African-American man in his fifties with salt and pepper hair and a permanent scowl. As he took his suit jacket off and draped it across the back of his chair, he looked at Sam, who was concentrating on his computer monitor.

"Catching up on yesterday's reports?"

Sam could hear the judgement dripping from Frank's statement.

"It was last night and it was late," Sam answered. "No one was here to look at it, anyway."

"Mmm-hmm," Frank nodded sarcastically. "It was late and you were out partying."

"It's called enjoying life, pal. You should look into it," Sam said. " And, for the record, I was off duty last night. I only answered the call as a favor."

Frank smirked and grabbed the coffee cup on his desk with a message that read DON'T TALK TO ME UNTIL THIS IS EMPTY.

Sam watched him as he lumbered over to the coffee pot, then turned back to his paperwork.

"Jesus, Sam," Frank yelled. "First one in starts the coffee. You couldn't even do that?"

"I was too busy with your mother," Sam yelled back.

Without turning around, Frank lifted his hand over his head and raised his middle finger.

Before Sam could respond, his office phone rang. "Lawson here."

"Detective Lawson, it's Carla Davenport, the new ——."

He interrupted her, teasing. "I know who you are, Carla."

Carla Davenport was the county's new medical examiner. She had recently relocated from New Orleans, and Sam had been building up the courage to ask her out ever since her arrival. She wasn't his normal type. Then again, his "normal" type was anyone drunk enough to go home with him at the end of the night.

Carla was different. From the confident way she carried herself to her charismatic charm, she was a woman who clearly had her shit together. It didn't hurt that she was attractive, too.

"You're calling awfully early this morning," Sam said. "What's up?"

"We need to talk about Joseph Reddington," Carla replied curtly.

"The fire guy?" Sam asked. "Why? What's wrong?"

"I'm looking at the body now," she answered. "This guy was dead before the fire even started."

6

The smell of a morgue is unlike anything else. There's the bracing antiseptics you'd normally associate with a hospital, combined with the looming odor of rotting death. It doesn't just enter your nose. It permeates your entire being and gets inside your bones.

Sam made a futile attempt at protecting himself by holding his breath as he pushed open the double doors. Carla was standing over the charred remains of a body, studying it the way a young kid would study an ant.

Sam exhaled and braced for the worst. Luckily, it wasn't as bad as usual. Burned bodies smell different, he noted to himself.

"Jesus," Carla said looking at Sam's bruised face. "What the hell happened to you?"

Sam shrugged. "Wrong place, wrong time."

He walked to the opposite side of the examining table from Carla, trying not to look at the charred body lying on the silver examining table between them. For some reason, the body looked even more horrifying this morning. Taking it out of its element of ash and burnt debris seemed to highlight the grue-someness of it all.

He shifted his focus to Carla, who was studying the remains, unaware of his gaze. Her dark hair was pulled back tightly in a bun, which made her features look deceptively sharp. Tall and lean, she looked like she could take anyone in a fight. She seldom smiled and carried a toughness about her that most people mistook as being standoffish and aloof, but Sam saw right through it.

"There was no smoke in the lungs," Carla said, finally looking up at Sam. "Which means he wasn't breathing when the fire started."

"So... heart attack? Lung cancer? Spider bite?" he asked. "Don't make me keep guessing. It makes me feel stupid."

"That's probably not too hard to do," she said with a slight smile.

"Did she just crack a joke?" he thought. Maybe he was starting to weaken that tough outer shell.

"See these fractures?" she asked, returning to the task at hand.

Carla pointed to the front of what was left of the head—not much more than a skull with patches of blackened flesh stuck to it. She then pointed to several cracks that ran across the skull before turning the skull to the side. Pieces of burnt flesh stuck to the table. Sam could feel his gag reflex kick in.

There was a section on the back of the skull—about the size of a wine cork—that seemed to be crushed in.

"It's called a contrecoup fracture," Carla explained. "He was hit on the back of the head so hard, the brain knocked into the front of the skull."

"Fuck me," Sam muttered.

"That's your cause of death, Detective. I'd say it looks like you've got a murder."

Sam was torn. On the one hand, he felt a little excitement at the prospect of investigating a murder case. It had been a long time. And it certainly couldn't hurt in helping him impress Carla. On the other hand, a murder investigation meant more paperwork and the chief breathing down his neck.

"You curious about what the murder weapon could have been?" Carla asked him, snapping him back to reality.

She didn't wait for an answer. "Probably something metal. Heavy enough to get the job done but light enough that someone could swing it to get the velocity needed."

Sam was only half-listening. He was already thinking about all the crap he now needed to do. First, he'd have to tell Chief Kaster. If Sam was lucky, his boss would pull the case on the spot and Sam could go back to wasting everyone's time. But if the chief didn't pull him, he'd need to get back to the crime scene before too much was tampered with.

He sighed. His day just got really busy and he was going to need more coffee.

7

The house had already been taped off by the time Sam got there. Forensics trucks were parked out front along with the Fire Inspector truck. A member of the K9 unit was letting a black Labrador out of his SUV—an arson dog trained to track accelerants.

Sam was surprised how quickly everyone had responded. He'd only stopped to grab a quick coffee. He looked around nervously for Kaster's brown Honda Civic, and his heart sank when he not only spotted it, but also saw Kaster standing beside it, hands on his hips, surveying the damage.

Kaster had probably been a brute force back in his day, but he traded in his toughness long ago. Now he was more a politician than a cop, more concerned with how a case would come across with the press. Or with the mayor.

Sam walked over to the chief. It was early already turning into a hot, muggy East Texas day.

"Glad you could make it, Detective," Kaster said sarcastically.

"I wanted to give everyone time to seal off the area," Sam lied.

Kaster never took his eyes off the house. "You didn't even bother looking around last night, did you?"

Sam just took the hit and walked toward the front door, Kaster right beside him all the way. A uniformed officer opened the door for the two men.

"You better hope to holy hell that all the evidence hasn't already been destroyed," Kaster continued.

"Hey, you thought it was an open-and-closed case, too. Remember?" Sam countered. "That's why you sent me."

Kaster walked ahead of him without saying a word. But the lack of a reply meant that the chief knew Sam was right. And that brought a smirk to Sam's face—one he quickly forced away before his boss could see it.

Sam trailed Kaster carefully up the stairs to the doorway of the bedroom. Two forensics officers were marking items and taking pictures. Crouching next to the ashen remains of the bed, just as he was the last time Sam had found him, was Tim Neiman.

"Hey, Tim," Sam shouted, a bit overly friendly. "Did you ever leave? Are you not able to stand up? You need help?"

Tim looked up at Sam and openly sighed in disappointment. Then he saw Kaster and stood up quickly, walking over to shake his hand.

"Hey, Chief. Good to see you."

"So, what have you found?" Kaster asked.

"Whoever did this sure did a good job of making it look like an accidental fire. The burn pattern has it starting in the bed, but we're checking for accelerants now."

"You find anything that could be a murder weapon?" Sam asked. "A baseball bat. A tire iron. A lamp. Something kind of heavy with blood on the end of it?"

Tim never even looked at him. He just shook his head in disbelief.

"So nothing out of the ordinary laying around?" Sam persisted.

Tim let out an exasperated sigh. "No. Nothing."

"Keep looking," Kaster said as he walked back to the bedroom door. "Lawson, come with me."

Sam patted Tim on the back. "Good seeing you, Tim. You take care."

He turned to walk toward his boss but stopped halfway, turning around.

"Hey, Tim. You keep a file of the particular way different arsonists start their fires, right? What's it called?"

"Their signature," Tim replied.

"Right," Sam said, nodding his head. "You think it would make sense to see if anyone has *this* signature?"

"There is no signature, Lawson."

Sam raised a finger. "Ah, but isn't that a signature of its own? What about arsonists that just burn beds?"

Tim nodded reluctantly. "It's possible. I can run it through the system and see if it pulls a match."

"Ha!" Sam laughed. "Pulls a match. Timmy with the fire humor."

"Fuck off," Tim sneered back.

But Sam didn't even hear him. He was relishing the fact he made a good call in front of the chief. For some extra brownie points, he made quite a show out of pulling out his notepad to write a reminder.

"Check with prison for list of convicts recently released," he said loudly as he wrote.

Kaster turned around, taking notice, so Sam explained.

"The victim was a prison guard so I'm guessing he had a few enemies. Maybe one of them was an arsonist."

8

The blindfold grew damp from her tears. She tried to listen for any sounds that could help her figure out who else was in the room. But loud, heavy metal music drowned out almost all other sounds. Instead, she could hear her heart pounding in her chest, her breath growing shallow and rapid.

She twisted her wrists, trying to relieve the pressure from the leather constraints wrapped around them. She had been forced to kneel with her hands bound together over her head. Her knees rested on what seemed to be the cold plastic of an exercise mat. At least he had spared her that comfort.

She could have yelled out, but it would have done no good. He probably would have liked it. Instead, she knelt in silence, engulfed in a claustrophobic panic.

After what seemed like eternity, she thought she heard footsteps. Then she felt a presence. He was standing over her. But he wasn't alone.

She shook her head violently and began to try and wrestle free from her constraints. She knew she was trapped. A warm, damp hand rested heavily on her shoulder. His hand. He caressed her neck *gently and she could feel his breath on her ear. It smelled like ciga-rettes and beer.*

"I have a present for you," he whispered.

Terror began to rise in her body, numbing each part of her as it climbed. Frozen in fear of what was coming next.

Then she felt him grab the front of her blouse and, in a sudden, violent motion, he ripped it open.

9

The interview room was hot. Higher-than-normal temperatures and oppressive humidity normally reserved for summer had slammed into this late fall morning. The AC was on the other side of the building so, by the time the airflow reached the small room, the vents let out nothing more than a lukewarm sigh.

Francine half-heartedly fanned a yellow legal notepad in front of her. From the circles under her eyes, it was clear she hadn't slept at all. But then again, it hadn't even been 24 hours since her entire world had been shattered.

Mitch was drenched in sweat. He rubbed his hands over his wet face and pulled them back over his short hair.

"How much longer do we have to sit here?" he complained.

Before she could answer, the door opened and Sam backed into the room, pulling a tall metal fan.

The mother and son watched in silence as Sam dragged the heavy fan across the floor. He didn't even look up at them as he scoured the walls to find an outlet. Finally, spying one on the other side of the room, he dragged the fan further, the screech echoing loudly. He plugged in the fan and the blades started spinning. As he aimed it at Francine and Mitch, they both took in the manufactured breeze as if it were life itself.

"Better?" Sam asked.

Francine and Mitch both nodded.

"Jesus. They didn't even get you any water?" he asked indignantly.

Sam walked back to the door and banged on it. "Can you guys get us some water in here?"

He turned back to the two sitting at the table.

"Sorry."

Francine smiled politely. Mitch did not. Sam pulled up a chair on the opposite side of the table and studied the mother and son.

Francine seemed understandably distant. She had yet to make eye contact with him, staring blankly at the wall behind him. She had a forced resolve about her, as if she was trying too hard to keep everything together. She sat a little too straight. Her breath was a little too labored. It looked like her outer shell was just one crack away from crumbling to pieces.

Mitch was a muscled-up ball of nervous energy. His left leg shook steadily, the heel of his foot tapping the ground as his knee bounced up and down. His upper body swayed side to side, like a boxer. His hands grasped nervously at each other, as if each one needed the other to calm it down.

"So... you all doing alright?" Sam finally asked.

Mitch snorted at the obviously stupid question. Sam nodded.

"Alright. Dumb question," he acknowledged. "I can't even imagine how hard this is for you."

Francine's eyes shifted down to the notepad in front of her. Mitch looked at Sam then back at his mother.

"Is this going to take long?" Francine finally asked. Her voice was firm and tired. She looked up at Sam. "There's so much I need to do."

Mitch reached out for his mother's hand. "Mom. We can get through this. It'll be okay."

She patted her son's hand and forced a smile.

"Do you know when they're going to release the body?" she asked, looking up at Sam for the first time. "Do I need to do anything? Who do I talk..."

Her voice trailed off, overwhelmed by all the responsibilities she knew now fell on her. Sam could feel her pain and he hated it. He had tried to pawn off this interview with one of the other detectives, but they shared his allergic reaction to consoling victims.

"Ma'am, I honestly don't know," Sam said gently. "But I promise you I will find out. And I'll help. Any way I can."

"We can't stay at my sister's forever," Francine said, thinking aloud. "What are we going to do about money? We relied on his job."

"He probably had life insurance, working for the prison and all," Sam offered.

Francine looked up at him. Tears had pooled in her eyes and were trailing down her cheeks. "I don't even know."

"We don't need his life insurance," Mitch blurted. "I'll get a job. You can get a better job. We'll be okay."

Sam couldn't help but notice the angry glint in Mitch's eyes.

"Do you know when we can get back in our home?" Francine asked "There are so many things I need. If they're not destroyed."

Mitch rubbed her back with one hand to help console her. He looked up at Sam, and Sam realized she had asked him a question.

"Uh, hopefully not long," he answered. "I'll talk to forensics and, as soon as they have all they need, we'll open it up to you. Assuming the fire department is okay with it."

Sam looked down at his feet, half out of embarrassment that he couldn't offer more. He decided to turn his attention to the son. He needed to find a way to connect with the kid. Then he remembered he was an athlete.

"So, Mitch. Your mom was picking you up from football practice last night?"

"Yeah?"

"What position do you play?"

Mitch seemed to welcome the change of subject. "Linebacker. All-state"

Sam whistled. "No shit."

Francine interrupted them. "Detective Lawson, why are we here?"

So much for small talk. Sam shifted in his chair so he could face Francine directly.

"Yeah. So, here's the deal. First off, I'm not gonna kid you. I'm not good at this kind of thing."

Mitch snorted and rolled his eyes.

"Yeah, I know," Sam continued. "I say the wrong thing. I make jokes at the wrong time. So, I apologize in advance. It's nothing personal. Just a nervous habit."

His confession got their attention.

"And I'm sorry you had to come down here and then get put in this sweat lodge. That's not fair to you. Or respectful."

Francine nodded politely. Sam accepted the invitation to continue.

"Did your husband have any enemies?" he asked.

Francine's brow crinkled in puzzlement. Mitch seemed to tense up.

"Why?" Mitch asked.

Sam studied their faces for a long time before speaking.

"I don't know how else to say this other than to just jump right out and say it," Sam said. "I think someone may have murdered Joe and then started the fire to cover it up."

Francine gasped.

"That's all we really know right now," Sam continued.

Francine tried to regain her composure. She spoke in forced, clipped words.

"Do you have any suspects?" she asked.

Sam told her he had hoped she could help him with that part, but she didn't know much. Her husband kept to himself and kept his work life very separate from his own life. But Sam pressed them anyway.

"I know you've both got a lot on your minds, but I really need you to think. Any enemies? Anyone who had a grudge against him? He worked at the prison. He ever talk about getting threats? Anyone that hated him?"

Mitch laughed.

"Are you kidding?" he said with a laugh. "Everybody hated my dad."

Francine shot a glare at her son and he shrugged back.

"What? It's true."

"Why is that?" Sam asked.

"Joe had a hard life," Francine interjected. "Working at that prison. It did things to him."

"I can't believe you of all people are defending him," Mitch shot back.

10

Sam's whole body shook as the metal prison doors clanged shut behind him.

"Jesus, guys," he grumbled. "Do you have to slam them?"

The prison guard manning the doors smiled at Sam and shot him the finger. Sam turned to Jeffery Hastings, the warden's assistant who was accompanying him. "You ever get used to that?" Sam asked.

Jeffery laughed nervously and pushed up his round wire-rimmed glasses with his index finger. He shrugged, pointing to a hallway on his left. He had a jittery quality about him that made him seem afraid of everything. He also afforded Sam a level of respect he wasn't accustomed to. A sure sign he was new.

The two men's footsteps echoed as they walked under the fluorescent lights of the long hallway that soon turned into a labyrinth of corridors. Sam wondered how anyone could ever find their way around. But maybe that was the point. It was a prison, after all.

Not that Sam wasn't familiar with prisons. As a kid, he'd visit them often to see his mother after she was arrested for drug possession. Sam was just nine years old at the time, but the bracing odor of stale cigarettes and bleach took him back there immediately.

As they rounded a corner, Sam saw a tall, gangly man with a thick moustache talking to one of the guards.

Warden Stivek.

Stivek was wearing a brown suit with a white shirt and a silver bolo tie in the shape of a cow skull. Dark brown cowboy boots peeked out from the hem of his slacks. His brown hair matched the color of his moustache and was fashioned into a very unfortunate comb-over.

"A country turd," thought Sam.

"Oh, good, you found me," Stivek said affably, walking toward Sam with his hand extended. His grin reeked of the kind of false sincerity that would make the warden a great politician. Or a used car salesman.

Sam smiled back and hid his instant dislike of the man as he shook his hand. They exchanged pleasantries, and the warden invited Sam to walk with him.

"Now what can I do you for, Detective?"

"I called you earlier."

Stivek nodded and sighed. "Oh yeah. You wanted a list of inmates released over the past six months. I'm gonna put that at the top of my list."

"You haven't already pulled it?" Sam asked, surprised.

The warden chuckled. "You only called this morning. These things take time. But we'll get right on it."

"It's a data file. On your computer," said Sam. "You literally just press some buttons."

The two men stopped when they arrived at another metal door. Sam felt a presence behind him and turned to see Jeffery had been quietly tagging along the whole time. After the three men walked through the door, Sam braced for the sound of clanging metal as it slammed shut. Even though he was ready, it still shook him to the core.

Sam could hear the echoes of muffled male voices from behind different walls. The right side of the hallway had a series of large windows that revealed some sort of breakroom. A handful of bored men in white jumpsuits were sitting around tables watching a small TV mounted in the corner. The other side of the hallway would occasionally open into perpendicular hallways that led to more metal doors. Those were the doors that led to the prison cells.

"I'll be honest," Stivek continued. "I don't know how any of that computer stuff works. I usually have my men do that."

"So, I'm assuming your men are on it, then?"

The warden stopped at a door and stared at Sam for a second, sizing him up. Then he answered with a greasy smile. "I really admire people who are passionate about their work."

He pulled a bundle of keys from a retractable key chain stuck to his belt and slid one into the lock of the door, pushing it open.

It opened into the concrete prison yard, and Sam squinted at the unexpected blast of sun. It reflected in a glare off of the spools of barbed wire circling the top of a tall chain-linked fence. The heat was oppressive. It battered down on him from the sky and rose from the gray concrete surface. Handfuls of prisoners sought refuge at a cluster of picnic tables under a shaded area. They looked up at Stivek and then at Sam. It was clear they didn't think too highly of their warden, and Sam instantly felt guilty by association.

"Come on, Warden," Sam pleaded. "I don't wanna be doing this any more than you."

"We'll be in touch as soon as we get it," Stivek said as he walked across the yard toward two guards standing near a basketball hoop. They both held rifles that were pointed toward the ground but clearly at the ready if needed. "Right now, I have a million things that need my attention. So, if you don't mind..."

"I understand," Sam said, still following him. "I just wouldn't want people to get the wrong impression."

Stivek unsuccessfully tried to suppress his worry. "How's that?"

Sam shrugged. "You know how people are. They read into everything. I'd hate for them to think you were hiding something."

Stivek turned around, his eyes narrowed. "Are you threatening me, son?"

"I don't have that kind of power," Sam said with a grin. "I'll get out of your hair. I've got another appointment anyway. Nancy Hellard. You know her? Channel 6 News?"

Stivek stared intently into Sam's eyes, sizing up the detective's statement. Stivek finally let out a loud sigh.

"Son, does Chief Kaster know you're here?" he asked.

"You think I'd come all the way out here on my own?"

The warden looked at Sam, thinking.

"I'll have something to you by the end of the day," he finally said.

Sam shook his head. "Sorry. I need it pronto. But tell you what. I need to interview some of your guards. While I'm doing that, Jefferey here can gather the files and I'll stop by and pick them up when I leave."

"I don't have time for this right now," Stivek said through gritted teeth, finally motioning Jeffery over. The young man practically jumped to his boss's side.

"Set the detective up in one of the interview rooms," Stivek said, never taking his eyes off of Sam. "And see if you can run that report for him."

11

Using his fingers as drumsticks, Sam banged out a drum solo on the metal table. The rhythm echoed off the cinderblock walls. As directed, Jeffery had set Sam up in one of the prison's interview rooms. Normally, this is where the inmates would meet with their lawyers or cops hoping to get some information. With the exception of the large two-way mirror along one wall, a small window directly across from it, and a small house fly sitting still in the corner, the walls were bare.

He recalled his interview with the wife and son, Francine and Mitch. He admired how she held herself together. He could tell she was terrified but she didn't want her son to know. He imagined how hard it must be. He knew what it was like to have your whole world pulled out from underneath you. He remembered how helpless he had felt and he found himself wondering if there was anything he could do for them. Did she have a job? Did she need one? Maybe he could help. He knew enough people. He could ask around for her.

"Sit tight, Sammy," he reminded himself. "Don't get involved. They've got family. They'll be fine."

He took a deep breath and brought himself back to the

present. He knew the warden was making him wait just to get under his skin. But there was no way in hell he was going to give him that satisfaction. So he kept banging away on the table.

When the metal door finally clanged opened, Sam masked his relief. A prison guard entered the room cautiously, and Sam stood to shake his hand.

"Hey there. You must be..."

"Charlie," the guard said. "Charlie Paloma."

"Charlie Paloma," Sam repeated. "I'm Detective Lawson, but you can call me nosy."

Sam flashed a disarming smile as he sat down. Charlie smiled back nervously. Even though he was probably in his late thirties, Charlie had a boyish quality about him. He was clean-cut and muscular with a sort of wide-eyed, earnest look in his eyes.

"Is this about Joe?" he asked as he sat in a chair on the other side of the table, the fly now buzzing clumsily between them.

Sam nodded. "You knew him?"

"We had the same shift. Partnered together a lot."

"Would you say you were friends?"

Charlie laughed. A little too loud. "I don't think anybody would call Joe a friend."

"You never grabbed a beer or anything? Outside of work?" Sam asked, finally remembering to pull out his notepad.

Charlie shrugged. "Yeah. I mean, sometimes. It was easier than making excuses."

"So what would y'all talk about?" Sam asked.

The answer was disappointing, but not surprising. According to Charlie, Joe only talked about football, his truck and women he wanted to have to sex with.

"He go out a lot?" Sam asked.

Charlie shrugged. "He'd go out for a drink or two but that's it as far as I knew. He had a family and stuff."

"I'm guessing you don't."

Charlie shook his head. "No, sir. I'm single."

Sam scooted up closer to the table and leaned forward. "Look. I need you to really think. Between you and me and whoever's listening on the other side of the wall," Sam raised his middle finger at the two-way mirror. "This wasn't an accident."

Color drained from Charlie's shocked face. "Holy shit."

He stood and started pacing nervously. "Shit. I knew something like this would happen."

"What do you mean?"

"We're guards, for Christ's sake. We're surrounded by some pretty bad dudes, and we're not exactly their favorite people."

He sat back down, bouncing his knee in an uneven rhythm.

"Should I be worried?" he asked. "Are we all at risk?"

"You know anyone who would have it out for Joe?" Sam asked, ignoring Charlie's question.

"Everybody had it out for Joe," Charlie answered, his voice still agitated. "I mean, no disrespect to the dead but... he was an asshole."

Sam smiled. "What about any ex-cons. Someone who got out recently."

Something seemed to light up in Charlie's mind but he immediately looked down, as if he were trying to stifle it.

Sam leaned forward. "What?"

Charlie's gaze was fixed on the fly, now walking across the detective's notebook. It was clear Charlie was weighing whether or not to tell Sam something.

Finally, he shook his head. "No. Nothing," Charlie said quietly, his eyes darting toward the two-way mirror. Sam could tell the guard was lying.

He knew something but was afraid to talk about it.

12

Mitch could hear them yelling through the walls of his bedroom. At first, he tried to muffle the sounds by burying his head under his pillow. He'd heard their fights his entire life but it never got any easier. In fact, now—knowing what he knew and seeing what he'd seen—it was even harder.

The thin wall behind his head was the only barrier between his room and his parents. He could hear way more than he ever wanted. He heard the way his father yelled at her. The names he called her. The way he talked shit about him to her. He heard it all.

He heard a crash and could picture perfectly in his mind the way his dad was throwing things off of the dresser onto the floor. His mother kept screaming for him to stop, and he'd yell back at her even louder.

Then the sound he dreaded most. The sound of flesh hitting flesh. Sometimes it was a loud slap but tonight it had a different sound. The asshole had punched her.

Mitch felt his blood boiling. He knew how hard his father could hit. His mother didn't deserve it. And she wasn't big enough to defend herself.

But he was.

Mitch yanked the covers back and stormed out of his room toward theirs, driven by adrenaline and hate. He stomped through the hallway and stopped in the open doorway of his parents' room.

His mother was cowering on the floor between the bed and the dresser. Her hands covered her face as she whimpered into them. His father stood over her, his right fist still clenched.

"Leave her alone!" Mitch yelled.

Joe spun around, his face contorted and twisted in a drunken rage. Mitch looked down at his mother. Her lip was bleeding, but it was the fear in her eyes that hit him hardest.

"What did you say?" Mitch's father yelled back, taking a step toward his son.

"Leave. Her. Alone," Mitch answered through gritted teeth. He felt his hands tighten into fists. His arms rose up to attack but Joe was already on him. Everything happened so fast it was a blur. Up until the moment Mitch felt the jolting pain of his father's fist.

13

Mitch took in the familiar smell of wet grass as he walked across the end zone of the practice field. The freshmen started practice at 2:30 while the varsity team worked out in the weight room. Mitch knew he would find Coach Robinson on the field. While he wasn't the freshmen head coach, he liked to watch them practice until the varsity team was ready.

As Mitch walked toward the coach, he passed a few of the freshmen players; all were pretending to be casual about seeing Mitch but it was obvious they were surprised. Mitch felt self-conscious as he felt their eyes on him. Like he was a ghost or something. It pissed him off and he could feel the anger building.

Not now, Mitch, he said to himself. You've got bigger things to deal with.

"Coach Robinson?" he said loudly as soon as he was in earshot of the coach.

The coach was engrossed in the action and didn't even notice Mitch as he walked up beside him.

"Hey, Coach," Mitch offered again.

The coach shot an annoyed glance back at the voice and

then spun around when he realized who it was.

"Jesus. Mitch."

Coach Robinson was in his sixties, but far from frail. At six-foot-five, he was easily 300 pounds. And his slick white hair seemed to be held in place with some sort of industrial-strength gel. He was wearing gray track pants and a wrinkled, untucked blue polo shirt with the Quinton Ravens logo emblazoned over the left chest. Mitch couldn't recall the coach ever wearing anything else, except for the all-weather team jacket reserved for cold nights.

"You doing okay, son?" Coach Robinson asked as he put a large hand on one of Mitch's shoulders.

It was the first time anyone had asked Mitch that since the fire. He could feel the emotions starting to rise in him, but he pushed them down and put on a brave face. Afraid his voice would betray him, he simply nodded.

He could tell the coach was relieved with the response. As supportive as he was with his players, he was not a touchy-feely guy at all.

"What are you doing here?" the coach asked. "You need to be home with your mama. Hell, boy, it ain't even been a day since it... happened."

"Can I play? This week?" Mitch asked quickly.

The coach wasn't expecting that reply.

"I don't know, Mitch."

"I just need something to be normal," Mitch blurted. "Me and my mom are living at my aunt's house... My dad... Everything's fucked up."

The coach nodded, still hesitant.

"I'll go crazy if I don't get to crash heads with someone," Mitch added. "Besides, my dad would be pissed if I missed a game."

The coach smiled weakly. He knew how true that statement was.

"Is your mom okay with this?" Coach Robinson asked.

Mitch nodded. "She understands."

It's what the coach wanted to hear. A big shit-eating grin spread across his face. Mitch knew now was the time to bring up the real reason for his visit.

"There is one little thing," he said.

The coach nodded, waiting for it.

Mitch took a deep breath and then just let it out. "I missed practice last night."

He could see the coach deflate a little, like it was a subject he would rather just leave alone.

"I figured you skipped off with Caleb again—which I don't condone." He pointed a finger at Mitch. "But I tolerate it because you always deliver on game day."

Mitch nodded. "Yeah. I was with Caleb. It's just that..."

He was hoping the coach would have filled in the blanks on his own, but he was just going to have to say it.

"I told the cops I was at practice," Mitch confessed. "I didn't want to get Caleb in trouble. His dad would kill him if he found out he skipped practice with me. I kind of panicked."

Coach Robinson nodded. He seemed to be buying it.

"It's just that... Well, they may want to check my story and if it sounds like I lied, they're gonna think..."

The coach held out his hand to stop Mitch from talking.

"No worries, son. You don't need that added grief on top of everything else you're dealing with."

Mitch let out a sigh of relief. That was easier than he thought.

"But let it be a lesson to you," the coach continued. "Even a little white lie can create a world of complication. Always go with the truth."

Mitch nodded. He felt lighter already. Thanking the coach, he turned to leave. Now he just had to find Caleb to get him to back up his story.

14

Sam sat at the bar and tried to appear as inconspicuous as possible. There were just a few bars in Quinton: Tony's, the one where most of the town hung out, a couple of shady joints just outside the city limits, and JC's.

JC's was the only bar on the only road to and from the prison, which made it the unofficial watering hole for prison employees. And, even though it was a Tuesday night, the parking lot was filled with cars and trucks that had Prison Employee stickers on their rear windshields.

Sam sipped a glass of beer, trying to make it last as long as possible. He needed to be able to buy Charlie a drink or two, and he had discovered too late that JC's was a cash-only establishment. And, after buying his way out of a bar fight the night before, Sam's cash flow situation was in sad shape.

He'd spent most of the day interviewing guards and prison personnel, and had finally wrangled the list of recent inmates from the warden late in the afternoon. Sam had Jeffery email the list to Detective Bannon, who'd be able to pass it along to some of the desk jockeys to check the list for arsonists or anyone else of interest. He had done more police work in the past eight hours than he had in the past eight weeks.

Still, it was his interview with Charlie that had been eating at him all day. The guard knew something and he seemed more afraid to talk than unwilling to do so. And that's why Sam was nursing a Pearl beer at JC's, in hopes that Charlie would show up for a drink. Maybe he would be more cooperative once he was out of earshot of Stivek.

JC's was nothing more than a long room with a bar that ran the length of it. There was a small TV in the corner airing the evening news, where a male reporter was standing in front of the Reddington house. There were still a team of trucks and police cars on the scene.

Sam leaned forward, trying to hear what the reporter was saying. Most of it was too muffled to make out, but the word 'homicide' jumped out at him.

How did they know about that? He had tried to keep the murder out of the press. He knew word would get around—especially with him out asking questions—but he was hoping he'd be able to buy a little time.

"Can you turn that shit off?" a deep voice bellowed from the other end of the bar.

Sam looked around to see who had said it. There were about a half-dozen men sitting and standing in clusters of twos and threes. Many of them drank in silence or among mumbled grunts of anger. After a day of having to tolerate the verbal abuses of protected inmates and navigate the bureaucracies of their own system, these men treated this pit stop on their way home as a holy rite. A place where they could shake off all the bad just so they could go home and try to act like everyone else.

The objection could have come from any one of them. And Sam didn't blame them. The last thing they wanted to hear after a day in hell was how one of their colleagues had literally burned to death.

Sam checked his watch. He had been waiting for almost an hour. He'd called the prison to confirm Charlie's shift and knew he'd be finished for the day by now. Sam was banking on him stopping by the bar after work, but was beginning to think Charlie had opted to skip it. He was just about to call it a day when Charlie walked in.

Sam watched Charlie say hello to his co-workers. He seemed awkward, like a kid who didn't feel he fit in with the rest of his class. And to be honest, just from meeting Charlie the one time, Sam could tell he was different. The other guards were tired and jaded men with chips on their shoulders. Charlie came across as more of a grown-up Boy Scout. He was the guy who would always try to do the right thing, which is exactly why Sam knew he'd be the one to talk to.

Charlie was laughing at something one of the other guards had said when Sam caught his eye. His smile fell immediately. Sam nodded at him, hoping it would be enough to let Charlie know he wanted to talk. After trading a few more barbs with the other guards, Charlie made his way down to Sam.

"What are you doing here?" Charlie asked.

"Hey, there!" Sam answered. "What a small world."

Charlie sat down next to Sam. "It's not that small."

"Charlie. Relax. What're you drinking? My treat."

"I... uh... just a beer."

Sam was relieved. He could afford a beer. He motioned at the bartender for two beers. Finally.

Sam shot the shit with Charlie for a while to build his trust. They talked about growing up in East Texas. Favorite fishing spots. The love/hate relationship Charlie had with his job.

"I was gonna be a cop, too," he explained. "But then my momma got real sick and I needed a job so I could take care of her. When the prison opened, I figured it would give me a paycheck and look good when I applied to the police academy."

"But one day led to another..." Sam said, nodding.

"Fifteen years later..." Charlie finished, chugging back the last of his beer.

Damn, he drank that faster than I had hoped, Sam thought. He motioned to the bartender for another, hoping he had enough money for a few more.

Charlie took the fresh beer and swigged back a large gulp. "I'm not young anymore. I probably couldn't even get in if I wanted to."

"Are you kidding?" laughed Sam. "You're in better shape than most of the guys on the force. Believe me, they'd jump at a chance for someone like you—especially with your prison experience."

"You think?"

"I could even put in a word if you want," Sam offered. He couldn't have asked for a better way in.

Sam sipped his beer. God, he hated sipping.

"And you know, helping out with this whole arson/murder thing could get you noticed in the right circles," Sam teased.

Charlie turned nervously toward the other guards at the bar. A couple of them were staring back at him with troubling looks on their faces.

Sam continued. "You wanted to tell me something earlier. In the prison."

Charlie shook his head. "No. No, I didn't."

"You did. I could tell. But we both know we were being listened to. That's why if I thought I found you here..."

Charlie chuckled and shook his head. "I wouldn't talk in a prison so you thought I'd spill my guts at a bar filled with prison guards?"

Sam looked down at the other patrons. As several of them glared down at Charlie and him, he began to feel the heat swell in his face.

"OK. I can now see the flaw in my plan," Sam said.

Charlie stared into his drink. Sam could see his mind whirring. He wanted to say something.

"Working at a prison can fuck you up," he finally muttered.

Sam wasn't sure how to respond. Luckily, Charlie kept talking so he didn't need to.

"You can't look at them as people. You have to shut off something in your head, you know? They can't be human. You can't be human."

Sam nodded. He understood all too well what Charlie was saying.

"The whole system is built on people not caring," Charlie continued. "You can't care."

The words echoed in Sam's head. The two men drank in silence until Charlie finally muttered a name under his breath.

"Manny Rodriguez."

He looked around to make sure no one was listening then went on to tell Sam that Rodriguez was an inmate who had done time for arson and murder.

"He had a bad beef with Joe. Got out about six months ago and high-tailed it out of town," Charlie continued. "But I know for a fact that he's back in town."

15

The "prison side of town" was filled with trailer parks, dilapidated homes and closed stores. Sam drove slowly, listening to the directions of his phone's GPS.

After talking with Charlie, Sam was able to track down Rodriguez's old address. Hopefully, the ex-con was a creature of habit.

Sam also had gathered some more information on his newly discovered number-one suspect. Turns out, Rodriguez had a record full of arson arrests. The guy was a regular pyromaniac. How he was not behind bars anymore was puzzling, but Sam had seen it so many times. Overcrowded and underfunded, whenever the prison needed to make room for new felons, they just pushed a few out with early parole.

"Turn right on Taylor Court," the GPS instructed Sam.

He made a sharp right on a street that he would have easily missed.

Even though it was 7:00, Sam had chosen to drive straight out to Rodriguez's house instead of waiting until the next morning. Why make the drive twice? Besides, he still had about an hour of daylight.

The trailer park could be better described as a trailer junk-yard. Five or six rusted, old trailer homes were scattered haphazardly off of a large U-shaped red dirt road. Tall pine trees kept the area in perpetual shade and blanketed the ground in rusty brown pine needles. A dog chained to a post in front of one of the homes announced Sam's arrival with loud, punctuating barks. Sam noticed a few people suspiciously peering through screen doors and windows. They probably didn't get a lot of visitors around here.

"Your destination is on the right," the GPS announced proudly.

Sam spotted the number 5 painted on a two-by-four in front of one trailer. Gravel crunched under his tires as he pulled into the empty driveway.

Some of the windows of the trailer home were broken and covered with cardboard. The front door was held open by a folding chair with no seat in it. The only sign of life was a white Styrofoam cooler that was nestled close to the front-door steps.

"Jesus," thought Sam. "He should have burned *this* house down."

Sam knew there was a pretty good chance a policeman would not be very welcome, and he was beginning to wish he had called for backup. But it was too late now. Sam took a deep breath and opened his car door. He stepped out slowly, with his hands raised in front of him.

"Rodriguez? You in there?"

There was no reply. Sam prayed there wasn't a rifle pointing at him from behind one of the windows. He could hear mosquitos buzzing around him and wanted to slap them away, but knew better than to make any sudden movements. He'd just have to suffer through a few bites. His skin began to itch at the very thought of it.

"My name's Detective Lawson. I just want to talk for a

minute," Sam continued. "That's all. Just a friendly, casual conversation. Then I'll leave."

Sam gulped and stepped toward the front door.

"I'm coming to the door. I'm clean."

Still no sound.

"No gun. I mean, I have one but it's not drawn." Sam realized he was starting to babble, but he also knew it was best to keep the suspect engaged. Even if it was a one-sided engagement.

"Sorry to stop by unannounced," Sam continued. "But I was in the neighborhood..."

Sam laughed nervously. He was now close enough that he could see inside the trailer. It was dark but Sam could see enough to tell it looked like someone had ransacked the place. Maybe no one was home.

"Rodriguez? You in there? You okay?"

When he heard the sound of bottles clanging together as they hit the floor, Sam jumped two feet back. But then there was silence again.

"You want to talk out here? Get some fresh air?"

"Go away," a deep voice finally mumbled from inside the trailer. Sam was both relieved and terrified at the same time.

"I just want to talk. Just for a second," Sam replied softly.

He heard the creaks of someone getting off a piece of furniture. Sam still had his hands in the air and, in that moment, felt more exposed than he would if he were completely naked.

Finally, a disheveled man shuffled through the shadows toward the door. Sam had read the files and knew Rodriguez was in his late twenties, but he looked much older. From the way he swayed side to side, it was clear he was drunk. Really drunk.

"Get the fuck out of here," Rodriguez ordered.

"I just want to talk. A few minutes."

Rodriguez teetered toward the door. He was holding a

garden hoe but, instead of brandishing it as a weapon, he used it to pop the lid off the Styrofoam cooler outside the door. He peered down and looked inside. Visibly upset with what he found, or didn't find, he turned and stumbled back inside.

Sam's eyes lit up and he smiled broadly.

"Hey! What's your poison?"

16

Sam had never been so happy he had made a detour at a liquor store after leaving JC's. Normally he wouldn't have been so keen on sharing his newly-bought bounty, but he knew it would be enough to gain entry into the highly-exclusive Trailer de Rodriguez. And he was always a big supporter of mixing business and pleasure.

He walked up the rotting wooden steps of the trailer home with a brown paper bag under his arm. As he stepped inside, he winced at the bracing ammonia smell of stale urine. Dirty clothes were thrown over the floor, along with beer cans, bottles, plates and rotten food.

Rodriguez was already sitting on the old orange couch that was covered with a stained brown sheet. He sloppily waved his hand toward a chair. Sam walked over, the floor creaking beneath him. He moved a pizza box, stirring to life an army of ants that had claimed the leftover crusts as their own.

As Sam cautiously sat down, Rodriguez pushed some of the fast-food bags, cigarette butts and beer cans off of the coffee table between them. Sam placed the brown paper bag on the newly cleared space and Rodriguez quickly reached for it, pulling out a bottle of whiskey.

"No tequila?" he muttered.

"I didn't want to assume..." Sam said, letting the words trail off before he got himself into trouble. "I hope whiskey's okay."

Rodriguez answered by unscrewing the lid and taking a big guzzle. He passed the bottle to Sam who raised his hand in front of him to decline. "I'll just have a beer."

He pointed toward his car outside. "I'm driving."

Rodriguez nodded and took another drink. Sam took the opportunity to get a better look at Rodriguez. He was drenched in sweat and, from the smell of it, hadn't showered in a few days. His long, jet black hair was pulled back out of his face into a pony tail. His stubbly beard was less a fashion choice and more a result of not shaving for a while. A gold cap sparkled off one of his front teeth and tattoos covered his bare arms. Sam could make out a dragon that blew flames down his left forearm and a heart on his right arm with the word "Maria" inscribed inside of it.

"Nice ink," Sam said, pointing to Rodriguez's arms. "Who's Maria?"

Rodriguez took another pull from the whiskey bottle. "You're here because of that shithead, right?"

Right to the point, Sam thought. He's a busy man. Got things to do.

"What shithead?" Sam asked.

"The fucking low-life guard that got roasted," Rodriguez said with more clarity than anything else he had muttered so far. "Joe Reddington."

"So you know what happened to him," Sam said.

Rodriguez shrugged. "I watch TV."

Sam looked around at the mess. "You have a TV?"

Rodriguez half grinned. "You think I did it, don't you?"

Sam bought some time by taking a swig of beer.

"Well, your name did come up," he finally admitted.

Rodriguez guzzled back more whiskey. Sam waited for him to say something else, but the ex-con offered nothing. He decided to just go with the obvious question.

"Can I ask where you were last night?"

Rodriguez chuckled and patted the couch. He told Sam he hadn't left his trailer all week.

"Were you alone?" Sam asked. "Anyone that can corroborate your whereabouts?"

"What do you think?"

Sam nodded. He knew it was a dumb question.

"You know this doesn't look good." Sam offered.

Rodriguez shrugged and took a long pull on the whiskey bottle.

"Nothing I can do about that," he finally said. "But I'll tell you one thing. Death was too good for that son of a bitch. If I had done it, you can be damn sure he would have suffered a good long time first."

17

Carla entered the last bit of data into her daily report and pressed "Save" on her keypad. She looked at the clock on her monitor and was surprised at the time. 9:05 p.m. The Reddington case was keeping her busy and she welcomed the break in her normal routine.

Carla was still adjusting to the slower work pace since moving to Quinton from New Orleans. She used to have a backlog of cases that she couldn't have caught up on even if she worked 24/7. Now, if she had any bodies at all to examine, they were normally car accident victims who needed their blood alcohol tested.

Not that she didn't welcome the less intense pace. Fear of burnout is exactly why she had moved to the sleepy East Texas town. But burnout had been replaced by boredom. Until the Reddington case came along.

She had spent most of the day trying to determine the murder weapon but hadn't gotten as far as she wanted. Tomorrow she would shift gears and start calculating the angle and velocity of the blow to the skull. From that, she may be able to get an idea of the murderer's height and whether he or she was left- or right-handed.

She was glad her skills could be helpful to the case. And she enjoyed the excuse to talk to Detective Lawson again.

Carla smiled at the thought of Sam. Sam was different than most of the other cops she had dealt with. She was aware of his reputation, but she hadn't seen that side of him and hoped it was more hyperbole than truth. Granted, he was definitely cocky. But it came with a sort of school boy charm. If nothing else, it was entertaining, which was more than she could say about any of the other men she had met in this town.

Maybe she just needed something to counterbalance her new, quiet country life. When she was working in New Orleans, her job was her life, so she never really developed any hobbies or extracurricular activities. Now she had nothing but free time on her hands and no idea of how to use it. She had started to fall into a rut. If anything, Sam seemed like a splash of cold water.

And if she was completely honest with herself, she knew she was drawn to Sam because he was exactly the type of guy she was always drawn to. The *wrong* kind of guy. The guy who was guaranteed to let her down. Her old therapist had told her that she picked them because it gave her an easy way out. She didn't have to worry about committing because the guy was going to do something to blow it before it ever got too serious.

But, like a moth to a flame, Carla couldn't help but be intrigued by Sam. At the very least, she wanted to learn more about him. Sure, there were risks. But with few other options, Carla was willing to take a chance.

She washed her hands in the lab sink and grabbed her bag. She knew Sam sometimes frequented Tony's, the local watering hole conveniently located across the parking lot from the police station. Maybe it was time she took herself out for a drink.

18

Sam sat at the bar, bathing in the AC, nursing a bottle of beer and thinking about Rodriguez. The arsonist was easily the most credible suspect he had. He was the kind of suspect an ambitious DA would be quick to railroad through the system just to show how tough they were on crime. Sam had learned the hard way how it worked. He used to bust his butt in search of the truth only to have his case smashed to hell because it was taking too long. They'd always yell the same thing: "The people demand justice!" But that was a lie. They didn't want justice. They wanted revenge. And they wanted it fast.

Sam knew he could throw Rodriguez to the wolves and probably get a medal for how fast he solved the case. Francine and Mitch could get some closure and Sam could go back to doing nothing again.

But there were too many things that just didn't sit right with Sam. For one, the man was a complete drunk and could barely stand up, much less overtake a big man like Joe Reddington. Also, there was no sign of a forced entry at the Reddington house, which led Sam to believe Joe let his attacker into his house—something he was not likely to do with a vengeful ex-inmate.

But if it wasn't Rodriguez, who was it?

Sam decided to leave Rodriguez out of his report for now. There were still too many unanswered questions and he wanted to be the one to set the pace, not some overzealous DA.

"Mind if I join you?" a woman's voice said, jarring Sam back to reality.

He was so lost in thought, he didn't even notice Carla Davenport pull up a stool next to him. Sam quickly popped out of his slump and smiled at her, struggling to come up with a quick and witty response.

"Looks like you already did," he replied. His attempt at clever had come out as rude. He back-pedaled furiously. "I mean, that's a good thing. I, uh, don't mind at all. Please, have a seat."

Carla seemed to ignore Sam's awkwardness and waved the bartender over. She ordered a beer and a glass then turned her attention back to Sam.

"Long day at work?" she asked. "My day was pretty dead."

She stared at him, waiting for a response but getting nothing more than a blank look.

"That was a joke," she said dryly.

Sam felt himself blush. "Right. Dead. Because it's a morgue. Sorry. My head's in the case."

Carla asked about the day's developments and he gave her a quick rundown—from interviewing the widow and son, to his day at the prison, then his bar date with Charlie followed by impromptu drinks with an arsonist.

"Jesus, how much have you had to drink?" she asked.

Sam brushed it off. "That was all in the line of duty. Doesn't count. And I didn't drink much because I had to be ready to possibly dodge a knife at any moment."

He told her more about Rodriguez. He knew he probably shouldn't be sharing details with her, but it felt good to talk to someone about the case. Truth be told, it felt good because it was her. He loved the way she looked at him as he spoke. It was intense but interested. And, away from the harsh lighting of the morgue, Carla was even more attractive. She was smiling more, and every time she did, he got butterflies.

The conversation shifted from his case to her time spent in New Orleans. They both shared a history of living in big cities and had jobs that exposed them to the dark underbelly of life. They agreed that the underbelly of a big city was just too much belly. You could easily get soaked up in it. Or worse, grow numb to it.

Sam's Houston job kept him in the bad parts of town. And, after his wife left him, his after-hours activities lived in the same shadows.

Carla hadn't let herself be swallowed by the dark side.

"You work with dead people all day long, you start to appreciate life wherever you can find it," she explained.

"So, what got you into the dead people business anyways?" he asked.

The question had been burning in his mind since he had met her. To him, a coroner was right up there with proctologist on the list of least desirable jobs.

"My customers never complain," she answered with a wink. "And they don't whine about their problems or ask for special treatment."

Sam was beginning to change his mind about the job's standing.

"But seriously, I like the puzzle-solving aspect of it," she continued. "I'm a detective, too. I just am working with a different set of clues. Plus, it keeps things in perspective. As bad as things get, it's never as bad as it got for them."

Despite what he had previously said, all of today's drinking was starting to catch up with Sam and he didn't want to make too much a fool of himself in front of Carla. Even though he didn't want to stop talking to Carla, he told her that he needed to call it a night.

To his delight—and surprise—Carla decided to leave at the same time. They paid their tabs and Sam walked Carla back to her car in the station parking lot. Standing by her car, Sam felt as giddy and nervous as a teenager. He wanted to kiss her so badly and she seemed like she wouldn't mind. But he was sober enough to question himself. What if he was reading her wrong? Why would someone as smart and attractive as Carla have any interest in him? He decided to play it safe and retreat before he made the wrong move.

He said goodbye and started to walk backwards. Did he detect a bit of disappointment from her? Maybe she had wanted him to kiss her. It didn't matter. It was too late now. He had either averted a bad misreading of a situation or had laid the groundwork for future possibilities. Either way, it was one of the few nights Sam had left a bar without doing some kind of damage.

"You're not driving, are you?" Carla asked.

Sam welcomed the chance to continue his conversation with her. He shook his head.

"I drink at this bar so I can walk there from the station," he said before pointing to a window above the hardware store across the street. "And I live in that apartment up there so I can walk home from the bar."

Carla laughed. It was too much. His old instincts kicked in and, before he could stop himself, he asked Carla if they could grab dinner sometime.

She looked shocked at first and Sam immediately wished he could take it back. But her surprise quickly dissolved to a wide smile.

"I'd like that," she answered.

Sam had to fight to keep his grin at moderately enthused. He told her he'd call her later when he had a better handle on his week, then left quickly before he could say anything else that could ruin the moment.

19

Mitch jumped into the truck, still pumped up about the game. The team's star defensive linebacker, Mitch had played one of his best games ever, being responsible for nine sacks and even an interception that he ran back for a touchdown. The coach singled him out after the game and awarded him the game ball.

"Was that a game or what?" Mitch exclaimed to his dad. "I was on fire."

"Let me see that," Joe said, smiling and pointing to the game ball.

Mitch handed it to his father proudly. His dad was always tough on him. Nothing was ever good enough. But no one could argue about that game.

He watched as Joe admired the ball, looking where all the players signed it. He imagined his dad displaying it front and center on the fireplace mantel.

"A lot of the guys are gonna hit the Dairy Queen to celebrate." Mitch said. "Can I go?"

Joe's smile turned south in an instant.

"I need you to come home and help me fix the sump pump."

"But it's night," Mitch argued.

"It's too hot during the day," Joe countered. "And don't argue with me."

"But that's not fair!" Mitch snapped, grabbing the ball back from his dad and slumping in his seat.

Joe yanked the ball back out of his son's hands. Before Mitch could even protest, Joe pulled out his pocket knife and stabbed into the ball, slicing a big gash in it.

"What the hell?" Mitch yelled in a panic.

Joe tossed the ruined ball into Mitch's lap. Mitch was stunned. He couldn't breathe. He could feel tears welling up in his eyes.

No. Don't cry. Not in front of him.

"Why did you do that?" Mitch asked in a shaky, unsure voice.

"Don't you ever talk back to me again," Joe blurted.

There was acid in his voice.

"That was mine!" Mitch heard himself yelling at his dad. "You had no right! That was mine! I earned it!"

Joe reached around and grabbed Mitch by the back of his head, shoving his face into the dash. Mitch felt the blood run from his nose.

"Are you deaf, boy?" Joe bellowed. "I said don't talk back to me."

Joe slammed Mitch's head on the dash again.

"You hear me?!?!?"

20

Mitch shook off the memory as he jogged along the side of Country Road 249. He had been taking early morning runs since he was a freshman. It was too hot to run after school. Plus, it gave him an excuse to avoid his dad before he left for work. Now it had become so ingrained in him that he would be half a mile into his run before he even started to wake up.

He focused on the crunch of his feet hitting the red dirt that ran along the side of the asphalt road. He found the steadiness of his footfalls oddly comforting amid the chaos in his life.

Mitch pulled his phone out of the pocket of his shorts to check the time. Almost 7:00. He picked up his pace. Mom would be getting up soon. His aunt and uncle had left before Mitch went on his run and he didn't want his mom to wake up alone. Besides, he liked making coffee for her in the morning and having it ready when she woke up. With all she'd been through lately, he needed to take care of her. God knows his dad never did that.

He promised himself a long time ago that he would do whatever it took to make things okay for his mom. To do anything he could to bring a little bit of joy into the miserable life she was trapped in.

And now she was free. She just didn't know it yet. He would have to help her see how much better life could be now. Now that he was gone.

He turned off the country road into the subdivision where his aunt and uncle lived. Nice homes and well-manicured lawns—it was very different from what Mitch was used to.

Mitch's aunt and uncle lived in a massive, two-story McMansion that sat right on Lake Puttman. Uncle Dale was a contractor and built most of the homes in the area, so he and his aunt were doing pretty good for themselves. Since they had no kids of their own, they were able to offer Francine and Mitch two of their spare rooms.

There were a couple of women power-walking up the street toward him, deep in a serious conversation. Mitch imagined it was about something that didn't really matter, like the unfair amount of homework their kindergarteners were bringing home or how one of their neighbors didn't pick up after their dog.

As he passed the women, he looked down at his feet to avoid eye contact. He found himself doing that a lot lately. It was something he needed to work on. Direct eye contact presents confidence, he remembered his coach saying.

Mitch was just two blocks away from the house now, so he picked up his pace to sprint it in. He was tired, but he pushed himself. He was actually enjoying the burn in his lungs until something made him slow down.

There was a strange car in the driveway of his aunt and uncle's home. Who would be visiting this early in the morning?

21

Mitch swung open the front door, still out of breath from his run. He turned to the living room to find his mother talking to a man wearing a prison guard uniform just like his father's. The two sat opposite each other: his mother on the couch and the guard in an armchair directly across from it. They both looked stiff and uncomfortable as they turned to Mitch.

Mitch glanced down at the coffee table between them. There were two cups of coffee already poured.

"Mitch, you remember Charlie Paloma," his mother said gently.

The man stood and awkwardly extended his hand to Mitch. He did look familiar but Mitch couldn't place him.

"Hi, Mitch. I just stopped by to pay my respects."

"Charlie worked with your father," his mother added.

Now he remembered. Mitch's father had always kept his work life separate, but he remembered once, when the two of them had grabbed a burger after a game, running into this guy at the restaurant.

Mitch shook his hand and looked to his mother to make

sure everything was alright. As if knowing what he was wondering, his mother nodded gently and smiled.

"I heard y'all were staying out here," Charlie offered. "I used to come out here and help your Uncle Dale with yardwork in the summer. It's on my way in to work so..."

He paused hoping that was enough, but Mitch just stared at him blankly.

"Anyway, I was fixing to leave a note, but your mom must have seen me walking back to my truck."

"You were awake?" Mitch asked his mother.

"I couldn't sleep so I came down to make some coffee. Then I heard something at the front door."

"I'm sorry, Mom," Mitch interrupted. "I should have been here. I didn't think you'd be up yet. I was gonna make you coffee."

"That's sweet, hon. But I know how to make coffee."

She smiled and both adults laughed. Mitch felt his face grow flush. He knew she was just teasing him, but he didn't like being the butt of a joke.

"Come sit with us," Francine said. Charlie returned to where he had been sitting and Mitch sat in another armchair next to it.

"Your dad talked about you a lot," Charlie offered to Mitch. "I guess you're quite the football player."

Mitch felt a surge of pride that quickly twisted into a strange bitterness.

"Never good enough," Mitch found himself blurting back.

"That's not the way I heard it," Charlie argued. "Mitch this. And Mitch that. He talked about you all the time."

Mitch felt confused.

"You were his friend?" Mitch asked.

"Well, we worked together," Charlie continued. "He wasn't an easy man to get to know."

"But you knew him well enough to know he was an asshole," Mitch sneered.

"Mitch!" Francine scolded.

"What?" Mitch snapped back. "You know it's true. This guy's painting him like he's father of the year."

"Your father could definitely be an asshole," Charlie interjected quietly. "But he did care about you. Both of you."

Charlie turned his eyes to Francine. She looked down, unable to face the words.

"Thank you for stopping by," she said as she stood up to signal the visit was over.

Charlie stood up as well. "Yeah. I've got to get to work. I wasn't even planning on coming in."

He turned to Mitch, who was still sitting. "It was nice seeing you, Mitch. Sorry again about... everything."

Charlie extended his hand to Mitch and he reluctantly shook it. Francine walked Charlie to the front door, and Mitch could hear them talking behind him.

"If there's anything I can do," Charlie said.

"Thank you. And thank you for the card," Francine answered gently.

Mitch heard the front door open and then shut. His mom walked back into the room.

"That was nice of him to stop by," she said, collecting the coffee cups.

"You know he was just telling you what you wanted to hear," Mitch said.

Francine nodded. "I know," she replied. "But I wanted to hear it."

"Why do you keep defending him?" Mitch snapped.

Francine took a deep breath and sat down next to Mitch. "Your father was a flawed man. He was far from perfect."

"He was a monster."

"You need to know that he wasn't always that way. Life beat him down."

Mitch stood up. "So, he gets to beat you? That's bullshit and you know it."

Mitch saw the words slap his mother across the face. It was the first time he had ever come right out and said it and he immediately regretted it. He knelt beside her and put his arms around her. He could feel her start to sob.

"I can never ask you to understand," she finally said through her tears. "Just know I always tried to do what was best for you."

22

Muted sunlight poured in through the dirty station windows. Not being hungover threw Sam off as much as a throbbing headache would have. It helped that he hadn't slept much—at least he was still battling morning fatigue.

The excitement of a pending date with Carla was partly responsible for his insomnia. That, and the conversation he had shared with Manny Rodriguez. His overactive mind had pinged back and forth between the two all night.

He unfolded the piece of paper he had stuffed in his pocket. It contained a list of restaurants where Sam could take Carla. Looking at it in daylight, he immediately scratched off several of the ideas. Nothing too pretentious or overly romantic, but nothing too casual. They had to have waiters. No ordering from a menu at a counter. He had some standards, after all.

He finally decided on Gable's, an old steakhouse near the police station. Not only was it convenient, but he was friends with the owner, so there was a chance he'd be able to run a tab and spend beyond his wallet. He decided to call later and make a reservation.

With his date plans out of the way, Sam returned his

thoughts to Rodriguez and how much hatred he had for Joe Reddington. At first, Sam had just written it off as inmate/guard animosity, but the more he thought about it, the more he suspected something else was fueling the hate.

As if on cue, Sam's desk phone rang. It was Charlie Paloma. He wanted to know how it had gone with Rodriguez.

"Did you arrest him?" Charlie asked.

Sam could sense the nervousness in his voice. He told him that he interviewed him but the ex-con was too drunk to offer any useful information—and certainly not enough to make an arrest.

"You didn't tell him I gave you his name, did you?" Charlie asked.

"Of course not," Sam replied. "Why? You think he'd come after you?"

Charlie told him that Rodriguez was dangerous and should still be behind bars. He was worried that the ex-con was settling scores with guards and that he could be a target as well. Sam assured him that, in his current state, Rodriguez didn't pose much of a threat to anyone but himself. He could barely stand up, much less hurt anyone.

"Do you know what kind of score Rodriguez had with Joe?" Sam asked. "The guy really hated him."

"Everybody hated him," Charlie replied. It was something that Sam was getting used to hearing.

"Something happened between the two of them," Sam pushed. "And I think you know what it was."

Charlie replied with silence, but Sam got the feeling he wanted to say something so he just waited. Finally, the guard spoke up.

"Ask Rodriguez," he said, his voice shaking. "I don't want to get involved."

Before Sam could ask anything else, Charlie hung up.

23

Charlie tossed his phone on a chair and sat down on the weight bench with a huff.

Charlie had inherited his mother's farmhouse when she passed. He had left most of the house and furniture as is, even staying in his room instead of moving into the master bedroom. The one thing he had changed was converting a third bedroom into a weight room. It was basic. A couple of benches, various mismatched free weights and a couple of short dumbbell and long barbell poles.

"Why didn't he arrest him?" Charlie wondered.

He shifted until he was straddling the bench and reached down to pick up a dumbbell loaded with a 40-lb. weight on each end. He began to curl the weight with his right hand, feeling the burn in his bicep. A good workout would get his mind off of things.

His early morning meeting with Francine and Mitch had thrown Charlie off. So much so that he drove back home afterward and called in sick.

Lifting weights was Charlie's way of relaxing. He carried a

lot of nervous energy and needed healthy ways to burn it off. He puffed out heavily with every curl of the weights, but his mind was still lost in thought.

"Maybe I should tell the detective the truth," he thought.

But he quickly shook the thought out of his head. He was already more involved than he wanted to be. If Sam Lawson was even half a detective, he'd find out Rodriguez's motive. The last thing Charlie needed would be to get caught up in the middle of that.

Charlie's imagination began to wander. What if Rodriguez found out he was the one who had given up his name? Would he come for him? But how would he ever find out? Detective Lawson had assured him he could remain anonymous and there was no reason to not believe him. Still, it couldn't hurt to be safe. He looked at the Glock 19 sitting on the chair next to his phone. He had made a habit of always having the handgun by his side and even kept it on his nightstand as he slept. He had even practiced grabbing the gun in the dark. Still, maybe he would also put some of those light-sensor spotlights outside. Just to be safe.

He thought about Francine and Mitch and wondered if they were in danger. He didn't know what the cops had told them or what precautions they were taking to protect the mother and son. However, he had noticed a security alarm system on the wall of their home when he had stopped by earlier.

He switched arms and began pumping the dumbbell with his left arm.

Charlie had regretted his morning visit almost immediately. Francine was polite to him, but he could tell she felt awkward by his unannounced social call. He should have waited a few more days. Or just mailed them a card. Why did he feel such a duty to stop by and pay his condolences anyway? It's not like he and Joe were partners that had worked side by side for years.

They weren't even really friends. In fact, Charlie despised Joe Reddington. As far as he was concerned, Joe was an obnoxious, corrupt asshole who got what was coming to him.

24

Sam felt relief as he stepped into the cool air of the restaurant. As the day progressed, so had the stifling humidity and, as Sam walked to the bright red counter, he pulled on the front of his shirt to air it out.

Jay's Fried Catfish had become Sam's go-to lunch spot since he moved to Quinton. Fast food catfish had been a thing in the eighties, but Jay's was the only restaurant still standing. Most people opted for the burger chains or the local diner, which meant Jay's was never crowded so there was never a long wait.

He ordered his usual—2 catfish filets, cole slaw, hush puppies and a large Dr. Pepper—then carried his meal to one of the red booths along the windows. He was just about to dip his filet in a pool of ketchup when a woman sat down in the seat opposite him. Sam immediately lost his appetite.

It was Nancy Hellard, the television reporter Sam had used to bluff the warden. By many standards, Nancy looked like a model. Her bleached blonde hair and full face of makeup was camera ready at all times. She dressed professionally, but with a sexy flair. And while her looks definitely helped get her on television, they didn't do much to get her taken seriously. In fact, Nancy couldn't seem to break free from the fluff pieces about colorful characters or pets that could talk. But she was ambitious and was always on the hunt for the big story that would give her national exposure. To Sam, that made her dangerous.

"How ya doin', Sam?" she asked.

Bitterness dripped off her southern drawl. She clearly didn't like Sam and had good reason. A few years back, they had gone on a date and, as most things associated with Sam usually went, it had turned into a disaster. He wound up drinking a little too much and made one too many wisecracks at another patron's expense. A few punches later, Sam was being treated by paramedics and Nancy was hailing a cab.

Sam was always surprised she never did an exposé on him. She had the power to destroy his career but, luckily, only used it as blackmail to get information when she needed it.

"Not today, Nancy," Sam muttered.

"How on God's green earth did Sam Lawson ever land such a juicy murder case?" she asked.

Sam was smart enough not to take the bait.

"Who said it was a murder?" he asked, taking a bite of his fish and chewing very, very slowly to stall.

"Don't play me for a fool, Sam Lawson," she said. "You know better."

Sam took his time chewing. He loved making her wait.

"Aren't there any cute kittens in diapers you should be reporting on?" he finally asked.

"Think of it this way. If you fill me in on this murder case, you're in control of it," she said. "Otherwise, I find out and tell the story my way."

Sam took another bite of catfish. She was right. Quinton wasn't a small town, but it was small enough that she was bound to find out the details of the case. If he gave her the story, he could at least stay ahead of it. And he needed a lead. Maybe a little press could help drum up some information. But he would only confirm that Joe had been murdered and the fire was a cover-up. Nothing about Rodriguez. Not yet.

Sam swallowed his bite and wiped his fingers on the paper napkin.

"Alright," he finally said. "But my name stays out of it."

25

After lunch, Sam made his way to the high school field house to meet with Mitch's coach. The unmistakable smell of a football locker room immediately took Sam back to high school. He smiled as he remembered hanging out after practice, talking smack and popping unsuspecting friends with wet towels. They would all tease each other about girls and how bad they played and make fun of teachers and coaches.

Sam had been a good player in high school and had even been considered for a scholarship. But without anyone really looking out for him, his grades were terrible and his attitude was worse. He wasn't good enough for local colleges to overlook his detention record. And, truth be told, he had no interest in going to college anyway. He couldn't wait to get out of school. Of course, as usual for Sam, he hadn't thought much about what to do next. He knocked around a series of jobs: gas station attendant, factory worker, cell phone salesman. He got fired from every single job he ever had and always heard the same thing: "You lack self-discipline and have a problem with authority." Finally, Sam had a genius idea. "If I have a problem with authority, why not become the authority?"

He knocked on the coach's closed door.

"Come in."

Sam tried to push the door open but a stacked pile of boxes blocked the doorway.

"Oh, shit," said Coach Robinson. "Let me get that."

Through the crack in the open door, Sam could see the coach stand from behind his desk and maneuver between piles of equipment and playbooks. He could hear the boxes being pushed across the floor just enough for Sam to squeeze in.

"Sorry for the mess," Robinson offered with a grin.

He extended his thick hand and Sam tried hard not to wince at the overly strong grip.

"You're the cop, right?" Robinson asked.

"Yes, sir. Detective Lawson," Sam answered as he waited for the coach to remove a stack of binders from the chair that faced the desk. "I just had a few quick questions."

Coach Robinson motioned to the cleared chair to indicate Sam should sit there, then he began slowly wedging his large frame around to his side of the desk.

"Sorry for the disaster area," Robinson said. "I don't clean up until the season is over. Just an old superstition that's always served me well."

"I don't clean up, either." Sam offered. "No superstitions. Just laziness."

The coach chuckled. "So, you have some questions?"

"Man, I have to tell you," Sam said, not quite ready to jump into the case. "Being in a locker room takes me back."

"You played ball?"

Sam nodded. "Tight end. Over at Black Rock."

The coach nodded in recognition. "They've got a good program."

"I mean, it was a long time ago. I had good knees and less gut."

The coach laughed again. "Didn't we all?" He pointed to Sam's face. "Looks like you been playing without a helmet, too."

Sam remembered his bruised face.

"Yeah. Sometimes the bad guys fight back."

That got a laugh out of the coach. Sam pulled his notepad from his jacket pocket, secretly congratulating himself that he remembered it before asking any questions. "I just have a few housekeeping questions about Mitch Reddington."

Sam noticed the coach shift a little in his seat.

"Fine kid," Robinson said. "I can't imagine what he's going through."

"Yeah. It can't be easy," Sam replied. "I'm glad he's still got the game."

"Football can teach you a lot and get you through a lot," Robinson said. "There's a reason it's the official religion of Texas."

"So, the night of the fire," Sam continued. "Mitch was at practice?"

"As far as I can remember," the coach answered. Sam noticed how he gulped after he spoke.

"It was just a couple of nights ago," Sam said.

The coach laughed again and waved his arm around the mess in his office. "Do I strike you as a guy with an organized mind?"

Sam laughed and nodded. "Do you remember anything about that practice? Anything unusual? Did Mitch come late? Leave early?"

"You played ball, right?" Robinson asked. "You remember what practices were like? Helmets on. Different units practicing different drills. There's a thousand things going on at once."

Sam smiled and nodded. "Glad to hear it's hard on the coaches, too. Practices used to kick my ass."

The coach smiled back, but then his face grew serious. He

studied Sam. A look of concern spread across his face. "You don't think Mitch was involved, do you?"

Sam shrugged and shook his head. "I have to consider all the angles, Coach. Just like you."

"Look, Mitch had some troubles," the coach offered. "Mainly with his dad. But he's a good kid. I can personally vouch for his character. He'd never do anything like... that."

"I totally get it. I just need to dot my I's and cross my T's," Sam explained. "If someone hid anything, for even innocent reasons, it could come back in a bad way. We have a suspect, but if it doesn't pan out, an overambitious DA could make our boy Mitch their scapegoat. I want to get ahead of that. So, if you know anything..."

The coach picked up a football and stared at it while twirling it in his hands.

"He left early Monday," the coach finally admitted. "I didn't even notice, but he confessed to it later. And he certainly wouldn't have told me if he was guilty of anything. He asked if I could keep it a secret because he had lied to the police in a moment of panic and knew it looked bad. He also didn't want to get a friend in trouble. That's the kind of kid Mitch is."

"Did he say why he left?" Sam asked, trying to hide his surprise at the answer.

The coach shrugged. "He and his friends did it all the time. I didn't like it, but it never affected their game, so I looked the other way. I'm not proud of that."

Sam scribbled furiously in his notepad.

"Do you know who he would have been with?" Sam asked.

"Caleb McConnell," the coach answered without hesitation.

Sam jotted down the name.

"This is helpful, Coach," Sam said. "You did the right thing telling me. Hopefully it ends right here with you and me."

"Mitch's dad was a mean son of a bitch," Robinson said without even thinking about it. "Obsessed with his kid's game.

Pushed him too hard. Pushed me too hard. I had to ban him from the playoffs last year."

"Why was that?" Sam asked.

"Yelling at the refs. At the kids—on both teams. Getting into fights with other dads."

"He got into fights? Physical fights?"

"Fists a'blazing. Mitch was mortified, you can imagine. I told Joe to stay away or I'd get a restraining order."

"And he stayed away?"

Robinson nodded. "He listened to his old coach."

"Wait. You coached Joe Reddington, too?"

Robinson laughed. "That's what happens when you stay in one place long enough. I've coached three generations here."

He reached into a pile on a bookshelf behind him and fumbled through some books before pulling out an old high school yearbook. He flipped through it until he found a picture and showed it to Sam. It was an action shot of a baseball player taking a swing.

"Baseball was Joe's game. Damn good third baseman. Good hitter, too."

Sam scribbled quickly to get it all down. The coach looked at the picture and sighed.

"He was even a son of a bitch then. Angry kid. And life just made him angrier. Sometimes, I feel like I could have done more to help him. Turn him around."

He slammed the book shut and tossed it back on the bookshelf.

"I've seen that kind of anger in Mitch, too," he continued. "But he channels it into the game. It's what makes him such a fierce player."

26

Francine felt a sense of dread wash over her. He was demanding she answer him, but she didn't understand his slurred question. She knew better than to ask again. That was a sure way for his impatient wrath to come down on her.

"Answer me, woman!" he yelled again.

He pulled himself out of his recliner and kicked one of the beer cans that littered the carpet around his chair.

"When is dinner going to be ready?" he demanded.

She felt a small sense of relief. At least she knew the question now. But she also knew he wasn't going to like the answer.

"I... I.. haven't started it yet. Maybe an hour?"

He stumbled toward her, obviously drunk.

"I told you I wanted to eat early!" he slurred.

Francine backed away from him until she was stopped by the wall. Her eyes welled up with tears and she began to hyperventilate.

"You're worthless," he growled.

"I was waiting for Mitch to get home," she offered weakly.

"Fuck him!" Joe yelled, knocking a vase of flowers off the counter to his side. "I said I wanted to eat early and you ignored me."

She began to shake her head, not in argument against him but in despair over what she knew was coming. She shut her eyes tight and covered her face with her hands. But Joe had walked up to her by now and slapped her hands away from her face.

"Look at me!" he yelled.

She could smell the beer on his breath as she struggled to open her eyes and face him. Why was it so hard to look at him?

She glanced up at him. The glare in his rage-filled eyes was too much and she looked away without even meaning to.

"Look at me!" he yelled even louder.

And then she felt the bracing sting from the back of his hand across the left side of her face. A bolt of pain shot through her cheek and her teeth rattled from the force of his blow.

She cried out but her ears were ringing so loudly she couldn't hear her own voice. As she slid down the wall, she began to sob. The corner of her lip burned and she tasted her own blood.

And then he struck her again.

27

Francine sliced the knife slowly and deliberately through the celery stalk. A good cook, Francine would normally cut a stalk of celery in seconds with a series of rapid-fire chops. But, since the fire, everything in Francine's life seemed to move in slow motion. Most of the time, she felt like she was operating on autopilot.

The sound of her sister's voice chattered in the background. It was just white noise to Francine. Ruth was three years younger than Francine and was the kind of person who got nervous with silence. Since she was a kid, she talked non-stop and, for her own peace of mind, Francine had learned to drown it out.

Francine hated the fact that her younger sister had to take care of her. Not that her sister would hold it over her. She had done much better in the marriage lottery. Her husband, Dale, was a successful contractor and they lived a nice, very comfortable life. Francine knew Joe was jealous of Dale's success. Even though they were often invited, he hated coming over and always made an excuse to not show. Francine knew better than to push the matter but she had always wished she could have spent more time with her sister. "Be careful what you wish for," she thought to herself.

"Francine? Hello?"

Francine snapped out of her thoughts.

"So you don't have any idea?" Ruth asked.

"About what?"

"About who did it. Aren't you worried?"

"There's nothing to worry about," Francine replied softly.

"Like hell there ain't. Joe was murdered and the killer is still walking free out there somewhere. Doesn't that scare you at all?"

Francine nodded. But, honestly, she hadn't even thought about it. She'd been too busy trying to avoid dealing with funeral arrangements and insurance adjusters. Dale had one of his appraisers take a look at her house, and his assessment that the house was irreparable was very different from what the insurance company's appraiser had said.

"Damage appears isolated to the one bedroom and roof with minimal smoke and water damage elsewhere." She couldn't believe someone had written that with a straight face.

Dale had offered to help her argue her case with the insurance company. But she had been putting it off. Between the insurance company, the house, funeral arrangements and bills, it was all too much.

She could feel her lip quivering again as her breath shortened. Ruth must have noticed the anxiousness in her sister because she quietly walked around the kitchen island and pulled Francine into a warm hug.

"I'm sorry," Ruth said gently. "I know I ain't helping anything. I just worry about you and Mitch."

Francine nodded her acceptance of Ruth's apology and then offered her own.

"I'm sorry I'm such a basket case."

Ruth pulled away from her sister to look her in the eyes.

"You are not a basket case. You're stronger than you give yourself credit for."

Francine shook her head in protest.

"You are strong enough to take on anything and you are NOT helpless." Ruth said, hesitating before she continued. "Not anymore."

Francine winced at the words. She knew what her sister was alluding to.

"I know it's hard right now," continued an emboldened Ruth. "But it's gonna get better. The Good Lord works in mysterious ways. You're gonna be better off, you'll see."

"Don't say that!" Francine snapped back. But in her gut, she knew her sister was right. It was her own guilt that was keeping her from admitting it.

"I'm sorry," Ruth said. "I shouldn't speak ill of the dead."

"I know you didn't care for Joe," Francine said. "And you had good reason. But you didn't know him like I did. You didn't see the good things he did."

Ruth turned her attention back to the chicken she had been de-boning. "Well, I saw enough of the bad things. The bruises. The black eyes. He doesn't get a pass for that."

"I admit he had a temper," Francine said, "But he was stressed. It was that damn job. I wish he never would have gone to work for the prison. It changed him."

Ruth nodded, not sure how to respond. She finally decided to deflect.

"I remember when you two got married."

Francine smiled at the welcome memory. "I was so nervous."

"Mama was so mad at you for marrying him," Ruth said. "But you didn't care. You were so in love."

Francine could feel herself blushing. "I was so pregnant."

"I do remember the way he looked at you when you walked up the aisle," Ruth said softly.

"He did love me," Francine said with a smile.

She squeezed Ruth's hand to thank her for the fond memory.

Why do we feel the need to only remember the good things about someone when they die? Why do we forgive them so quickly? Grudges turn to guilt. Hatred turns to sorrow. We assure ourselves that they found their way to heaven, even though we know their life was on a fast track to hell. Is it survivor's guilt? Or just a part of our innate need to appreciate what we no longer have?

Either way, Francine was drowning in a sea of conflicting emotions. Sadness. Despair. Loneliness. Relief. Hope. Anger. And guilt.

28

Sam stopped outside of the morgue doors to collect himself. This time, it wasn't so much the thought of the dead bodies in there, but the woman that was very much alive. The fact that he was visiting the morgue on purpose said a lot about how interested he was in Carla. Of course, he would never tell her that. He knew enough to play it cool. Women hate desperation and they can smell it a mile away. In fact, even though he had wanted to see her first thing, he purposefully waited until after lunch.

He was hoping she still wanted to go out with him. What if she had just agreed to be polite? What if she had thought about it and changed her mind? He was so glad he had official business to discuss.

When they had talked the night before at the bar, Carla had offered to help Sam out and he actually had something she could do. Sam needed to go through all of Joe Reddington's financial records, and the mere thought of it gave him a headache. There were a thousand things Sam would rather do than spend hours and hours reading over bank records and credit card statements. But Carla was stuck in a morgue that was dead—literally. She was starving for anything to do. She had said it herself. He wasn't taking advantage of her offer, he was doing her a favor, right?

He took a deep breath and pushed open the morgue doors. Immediately, the familiar butterflies in his stomach jumped to life.

She was sitting on a stool behind a laptop and looked up at him with that big smile. He loved the way her nose crinkled when she smiled. She looked glad to see him. That was a good sign.

He walked over and awkwardly waved at her. He decided to keep it professional. No hugs and definitely no kisses. But a handshake seemed too formal and he somehow landed on a half wave before shoving his hands in his pocket like a middle school kid.

Carla smirked at his awkwardness and teased him by waving back.

"How's the search going?" he asked, trying to direct her attention away from him.

"I can see why you pawned this off on me," she said, rolling her eyes. "But I'm actually glad you're here. I think I may have found something."

Carla filled Sam in on her search. The Reddingtons were a very frugal family. They didn't have a lot of money so they didn't spend a lot. Consequently, the bank records were boringly typical. Groceries, gas, bills and an occasional ATM withdrawal. But nothing of consequence. The credit card statements were turning out to be just as boring. But luckily, the cards were all pretty close to being maxed out so there wasn't a lot of room for purchases.

"But there was this one charge," she said. "It just kind of sticks out."

She turned the laptop around so he could see the screen.

He scanned a digital credit card statement, trying to find what she was looking for.

"It feels kind of wrong to be doing this," she said. "I mean, like it's a real invasion of privacy."

"Yeah, well in my experience," he replied, "dead people don't care as much about that."

"Yeah," she countered. "But his family might."

He finally saw what caught her attention. It wasn't just the amount of $99. That was way more than any other charge on the statement. It was what the charge was billed to:

FanDung.

"What the hell is FanDung?" Sam muttered out loud.

"That's where it gets really interesting," Carla said with a tinge of excitement in her voice. "I looked it up. It has to be this."

She showed him the screen on her iPhone that had a Google results page open. He looked at the top entry:

Fantasy Dungeon.

And it was local.

29

The house may have matched the address but it did not match Sam's expectations. It looked no different than any other farmhouse Sam had ever seen. He was half-expecting a garish building painted pink and black with an XXX neon sign flashing on the roof. He was more than slightly disappointed.

A gravel driveway cut across an acre of land and led Sam to a modest, two-story farmhouse with white wooden panels and gray shutters.

After discovering the suspicious purchase, Sam had called the number on the website and spoke to a man named Dennis Mosely. Dennis seemed cautious on the phone. He was used to getting calls from all kinds of weirdos. When Sam had first mentioned he was a cop, Dennis had nearly hung up. But Sam convinced him that he was just following a lead and he would be discreet. Hell, he had told Dennis, if he had known a place like this existed in the area, he'd probably be buying a membership himself. Dennis finally relented to an interview but only in person. He had given Sam directions and asked that he come before 6 p.m., as that was when "members" would start arriving.

Sam pulled to a stop in front of the house. He stepped out of his car and was greeted by the sound of clucking chickens and a loud moo from one of two brown cows. Just a typical farm, Sam thought.

He knocked on the door and heard footsteps approaching from the other side. The door opened slowly to reveal a large man who looked to be in his fifties, with short, salt-and-pepper hair and a darker, close-cut beard. He was wearing jeans and a plain black T-shirt. You would never know from looking at him what kind of establishment he ran.

Sam introduced himself, and Dennis looked around to make sure Sam was alone before letting him in.

The inside of the house was just as traditional as the outside. A small hallway led into a modest living room, where an old light-green couch and two brown La-Z-Boy recliners sat semicircle over a large, oval braided area rug.

Without a word, Dennis led Sam through the living room into the eat-in kitchen that appeared to double as the office, ducking his large frame as he passed through the doorway. Papers and a laptop sat on the round, chrome-trimmed kitchen table. Dennis sat down and motioned for Sam to do the same.

The only sound was the steady ticking of the kitchen clock, and the silence was making Sam uncomfortable. He had been waiting for Dennis to speak first, mainly because he wasn't sure what to say. But his nervous energy was getting the best of him.

"Your house looks so normal," he found himself blurting out.

Dennis lit a cigarette and held one out for Sam, who shook his head. The big man took a long drag and studied Sam. He finally cracked a smile.

"This is my living room and kitchen."

His voice was deep and mellow. It was the one thing about him that seemed to match what Sam expected from the manager of a sex club.

"The dungeon is downstairs," he continued. "More play-rooms are upstairs."

Playrooms.

"You want a tour?" he asked.

"Maybe later," Sam answered.

He wanted a tour more than anything. He was dying to know what was in a "playroom," and was even more curious about a "dungeon." But, before he could give into temptation, he asked Dennis about the $99 charge from Joe Reddington.

"Who's Reddington?" Dennis asked with little real interest.

"Joe Reddington," Sam answered. "He's the guy who burned in the house fire a few days ago."

Dennis took another long drag from his cigarette then nodded his head. "Oh, yeah. That guy."

Sam waited for him to say more, but Dennis offered nothing. Jesus, it's like pulling teeth with this one, he thought.

"I'm guessing he was a member here?" Sam finally prodded.

Dennis scratched his head. "Yeah. That's what the $99 charge was for. It's just that... that kind of stuff is sort of confidential, you know?"

Sam nodded. "I get it. And why start pulling out all the skeletons in a dead man's closet, right? But we have reason to believe his death wasn't an accident and the killer could possibly be someone from this club."

Sam was hoping the veiled threat would be enough. This guy was too big and Sam didn't think his face could take another punch.

Dennis turned his head to blow out smoke, never taking his eyes off Sam. "I don't need any publicity," he said.

"Look, this is just a conversation between you and me," Sam assured him.

Dennis put out his cigarette and opened his laptop. He typed a few things on the keyboard and started scrolling.

"Yep. Joe Reddington. Member for a little while. Looks like I kicked him out."

Sam thought it was odd that he didn't mention that right off the bat.

"I remember him now. He was being an asshole to some of the other guests," Dennis said. "This is all consensual fun between really nice folks, but sometimes someone shows up that don't understand "no." Or don't care. I warned him a couple of times and... three strikes, you're out. Never seen him since."

"How long ago was that?" Sam asked.

Dennis checked the laptop. "About a year ago."

"How long had he been coming here?"

"They'd been coming about six months," Dennis answered.

"They?" Sam was surprised by the word.

"Oh, yeah. Single men aren't allowed. They all bring partners. Sometimes the same one, sometimes different."

"And what about Joe?" Sam asked, finally remembering to pull out his notepad to take notes.

"Always the same lady. He said it was his wife."

Sam looked up.

"You said his wife?"

Dennis nodded. "That's what he said, at least."

He looked down at his laptop.

"She went by Francine, but a lot of guests use fake names."

Sam's head was spinning. "What can you tell me about Francine?"

Dennis lit another cigarette, thinking. "I don't remember much. A lot of people come through here. And I'm usually preoccupied."

"Anything at all would be helpful."

Dennis thought for a bit and then nodded his head. "I remember Joe would share her with other guys."

Sam almost had to check to make sure his jaw hadn't hit the floor. Francine? How could he have someone pegged so wrong.

"And she liked that?" he asked.

Dennis nodded. "Everyone signs a letter of consent."

He stood up with a groan and walked to a file cabinet. Sam was impressed by how organized this dungeon master was. Dennis flipped through files and pulled out a slip of paper, handing it to the detective.

Sam stared at the signatures at the bottom of the release form: Joe Reddington and Francine Reddington.

"I can't even imagine," Sam said without thinking.

"You'd be surprised," Dennis said with a chuckle.

"And she was into it?" Sam asked.

"She signed the form," Dennis said pointing at it. "There's a lot of role play that goes on in here. People acting like they like it or don't like it. Lines get blurred in the fantasy. That's why I started getting these consent forms. And everyone keeps an eye on everyone. They use safe words. If someone seems like they're really not liking something, we check it out."

Sam started to write something down but couldn't figure out what to write. He finally just scribbled: WTF???

"Anything else you can tell me about either of them?" Sam asked.

Dennis shook his head. "I remember her being quiet and nervous. He was loud and an asshole. That's about it."

Sam stared at the consent form in disbelief. He noticed a third signature at the bottom: it was just the letter M.

"Who's that?" Sam asked.

Dennis looked at the bottom of the form and nodded. "That's me. It's my initial."

Sam noticed a newspaper sitting on top of the file cabinet and asked Dennis if it was today's issue. Dennis reached for the paper and handed it to Sam. Sam had hoped for an article on the fire and, fortunately, there was one on the front page. He scanned the article and flipped to another page where the story continued.

"This ain't no library, mister," Dennis said.

Sam laid the open paper down on the table and pointed to a cluster of photographs next to an article. One was of the burnt Reddington house. Another was a family portrait of Joe, Francine and Mitch.

"Is that her? Is that Francine?" Sam asked.

Dennis nodded. "Oh, yeah. That's definitely her."

30

Francine walked down the stone path toward the porch swing that sat near the lake's edge. It had become her favorite spot since staying with her sister: secluded enough that she could be unbothered, but still within sight of her family if she started to feel overwhelmed or panicked.

It was the perfect place to talk to Detective Lawson.

She looked back at him as they walked and pointed to the porch swing.

"Is this okay?" she asked.

He nodded with the same uneasiness she had noticed when he had called to meet with her. It was like he knew something. And it was beginning to agitate her.

When he arrived, he'd asked if they could talk in private, which is why she was bringing him to the porch swing. It was early evening and her sister was expected home any moment. She didn't want Ruth to walk in on whatever conversation she was about to have.

Francine sat down, staring at the lake in front of her. A light breeze blew in over the water and she pulled her sweater tightly around her. The sun was hanging low in the sky and reflected off the blue water. Water diamonds. That's what she and her sister had called the sparkles on the lake when they were kids.

The bench swayed and Detective Lawson sat down next to her.

"It's beautiful out here," he said, tapping his legs with his fingers.

"It helps me forget about everything," she replied. "Something about being out here makes everything else melt away."

The detective nodded. And, after an awkward silence, he finally started talking. As soon as she heard the word "Dungeon" things became foggy. He was still talking, but she could barely hear him. Her heart pounded in her head. Feeling like her lungs could not take in enough air, she began to gasp in shallow dizzying breaths.

She had tried so hard to forget about that episode in her marriage. She had prayed it would be buried with her husband, but now here was a complete stranger telling her he knew about it. And it was all happening so fast.

"Are you alright?"

She heard the question but couldn't answer. It was all too much. She needed to get away. But where could she go? Her safe place now had her trapped by the water's edge.

"Do you want me to get you some water or something?"

"Collect yourself," Francine thought. "Just get this over with. Maybe it was nothing. Maybe it could be buried again."

She started taking deep breaths and slowly felt herself calming down.

"I'm so sorry," Sam said gently. "I know this is a weird thing to talk about. Especially with a stranger. If it helps, it's really awkward for me, too."

Francine felt small and humiliated, just like she did when

Joe had forced her to go to that place. She finally mustered up enough oxygen to answer.

"I'm sorry," she managed, the words catching in her throat. "I had hoped that would stay private."

"No one else knows," Sam assured her. "It's not in any report or anything and I'll keep it private if I can. I'm really sorry I even have to bring it up."

She could feel him looking at her. Was he judging her? Was he thinking she was something she wasn't?

"He made me go," she heard herself saying. "I didn't want to. I never wanted to."

"He forced you?" Sam asked.

She nodded. "He said it would be good for our marriage and I needed to do what he said. I tried to talk him out of it. I begged him. But he insisted."

"You signed a consent form," Sam said, puzzled.

She nodded. "I had to. I didn't want to make him mad. And once we were... inside, he told me I had to do whatever he said..."

Blackness began to threaten the edges of her peripheral vision. Flashes of repressed memories came flooding into her mind. The strange men. The way they had looked at her. Groped her. Used her. And the way Joe smiled through it all.

He would blindfold her and make her kneel in a room, strange men encircling her. Then he would rip her blouse open, exposing her. Humiliating her. And, because she was afraid of him, she let him.

She felt a hot rush of nausea and turned away from Sam to vomit. Her body trembling, she collapsed in heaving sobs. Sam wanted to comfort her but didn't know what to do. His awkwardness was almost childlike, and Francine couldn't help but feel sorry for him. It turned out being exactly what she needed. A distraction. She started to gather her composure.

"I'm so sorry I brought this up," Sam said. "I feel like an asshole."

"How did you find out?" Francine asked, suddenly feeling paranoid. "Who told you?"

"I was following up on another lead. About your husband," he answered. "I just found out about you by accident. Nobody else knows."

Francine nodded. Sam wanted this entire conversation to end. But he needed to know something else

"You said he made you go. Were you afraid of Joe?"

She felt a cold tear roll down her cheek as she slightly nodded.

"Did you... have a reason to be afraid?"

More tears trailed down her cheeks. She wanted to answer him. She wanted to tell him how her husband had punched her in the face. How he once broke her arm in a fight. How he would slam her head down on the kitchen table. Or burn cigarettes out on her forearm. She wanted to tell him what a monster Joe had been. She wanted to tell him everything. But saying the words made it all more real.

She saw Sam's concerned look out of the corner of her eyes and mistook it for judgement.

"Don't think I didn't want to leave. I tried. But he took pictures when we were there. He told me if I ever left him he'd post them on the internet. I didn't care about me. But I couldn't do that to Mitch."

A whirlwind of emotions started to rise in her. She felt like she was going to burst into tears. Then it happened. That "thing" clicked inside her. The way it always did when she started to feel too threatened. All the bitterness and anger started to close in on itself. Her jaw tightened and she clinched her fists tight.

"He put me through hell," she said through gritted teeth. "He deserved to die."

She instantly regretted saying the words out loud. She felt ashamed. Guilty. Her rage quickly flipped to panic—like a little girl who just got caught doing something wrong.

"I think you need to leave."

31

Sam made a conscious effort to chew his steak slowly with his mouth shut. He normally ate alone, so he had no need for manners. But tonight he wanted to make a good impression on Carla. Wolfing down his food would certainly not do that.

Not wanting to wait, Sam had asked her out that very night and, luckily, she agreed. After leaving Francine, Sam had gone home and taken a quick shower, then changed into a fresh blue shirt and black jeans. He knew Carla would be coming right from work so he didn't want to overdress. But between the locker room and the sex club, he felt he needed to wash away a lot of the day.

Gable's was a decent enough restaurant. From the red carpet to the beige stucco walls, the place looked like it had been pulled right out of the seventies. But they used cloth napkins, which put it a class above most places in Quinton. For real fine dining, most folks traveled about an hour northeast to Tyler. But Sam figured that would be a little too much for a first date. Besides, a restaurant in Tyler wasn't likely to cover the tab until Sam's next paycheck, which is what Sam's friend who owned Gable's had agreed to do.

Knowing he didn't have to worry about paying for every-thing, at least for tonight, Sam was splurging. In addition to his ribeye steak, Sam had ordered two glasses of red wine and encouraged Carla to get anything she wanted because it was a special night.

Carla had come straight from the office, but, without her lab coat, she looked like she had dressed special for the occa-sion. Sam thought she seemed more attractive than ever. Had the lab coat made that big of a difference? Or was he looking at her through a different lens now.

After small talk about the day and the weather, Carla asked Sam how it went at Fantasy Dungeon. Talking about a sex club on his first date made Sam squirm in his seat, but Carla's matter-of-factness about the subject put him at ease.

He told her about how Joe had been kicked out of the club for being too aggressive. About how he had forced Francine to go. About his conversation with her and his suspicions of abuse. Carla was horrified.

"That poor woman," she said. "But it certainly gives her motive."

"Honestly, the more I talk to people," he said, "the more I realize everyone's got a motive. The son, Mitch? He lied about his alibi and he's got plenty of motive. And there's the ex-con, Manny Rodriguez. He's got a motive and the right skill set. The more I dig, the more suspects I find. It's turning into a real mess."

"What about the murder weapon? Have you found anything that could have been the murder weapon?" she asked.

Sam shook his head. He told her that they had done a complete search of the house and found nothing suspicious.

"Well, nothing suspicious that also looked like it had been used to bludgeon a man to death," Sam joked.

"Have you been back to the crime scene?" she asked.

Sam shook his head no and noticed a look of dismay on her face.

"You're going back, aren't you?" she asked. "There has to be some evidence there. Something that was overlooked."

Sam assured her he was. But he was lying. He honestly hadn't even given it a thought. Forensics had combed the place over. What more could he add?

"I mean, I'm not telling you how to do your job. You're the detective," Carla said, slightly embarrassed. "If it were my case, I'd want to see it all for myself, you know? But I'm just weird that way. I get obsessed with stuff if you haven't noticed."

Sam smiled and assured her that no bounds had been overstepped. "I used to get obsessed, too."

Sam told her how his job had swallowed him whole at one point and how it cost him his family.

"You know what the kicker is?" he asked. "For everything you sacrifice, you don't even make a dent in it."

Carla looked into his eyes. "That's why you left Houston?"

"It's easier not to care about anything when there's nothing to care about," he said with a shrug. "It was easy here. Or at least it used to be."

"I think you're full of shit," she said matter-of-factly.

Sam was shocked but he couldn't help but laugh.

"You may have some people fooled, Sam Lawson, but I see right through you," she continued. "You care more than you let on."

She winked at him and smiled mischievously. He felt his heart do a triple back flip in his chest. It was good to be able to talk things through with someone who didn't yell at him or roll their eyes. And Carla was obviously very smart. She'd probably have made a great detective if she didn't like dead people so much.

They spent the next hour talking about all kinds of things. Their past jobs. Their favorite cases. Sam loved the way she laughed. In fact, he was finding that he liked pretty much everything about her. And she seemed to connect with him, too.

After dinner, he walked her back to her car in the station parking lot again. But this time, as she stood in front of her car, he stepped closer. He found his arms circling her waist and pulling her to him.

"I had a wonderful time, Detective Lawson," she said softly.

He answered with a gentle kiss. Her lips felt soft and warm as they lightly grazed against his. He leaned in to kiss her again but she leaned back playfully.

"Let's save the good stuff for when we're not in a parking lot," she said with a wink.

He laughed and nodded, too tongue-tied to jumble together any words. She got in her car and rolled down her window, and he leaned down and kissed her again.

"This is the part where I would normally try to charm you back to my place," he said. "But I'm heading back to the crime scene to see what else I can dig up."

He saw the spark in her eyes when he said it. *That'll guarantee a second date*, he thought to himself as he watched her drive off.

He walked back to his car on Cloud 9. Of course, he had no real intention of going back to the house. What could he possibly find there? But, as he settled behind the wheel, he thought about what she had said.

"If it were my case, I'd want to see it all for myself."

Clearly, his reputation had not made it down to the morgue. She actually believed in him. He couldn't remember the last time that had happened.

Maybe he should take a look. Maybe he could find something the others didn't. He was a detective, after all. Used to be a damn good one. He smiled as he started the ignition, thinking about how good it would feel to actually solve this murder.

32

Sam drove to the Reddington house, still high off his kiss with Carla. The scent of her perfume lingered on his clothes. As he turned on to Reddington's street, he found himself replaying the evening. He couldn't recall the last time he had not wanted a date to end. Normally, he couldn't wait to get away—even if things seemed to click. But the evening had flown by with Carla. And, while he was proud of himself for calling it a night without trying to sleep with her, he also half-regretted it. He was left to imagine how soft her skin must be. How good she would feel in his arms.

The sight of the charred house snapped him out of his fantasy. Because of the water damage, the power had been shut off to the house, so it was pitch black. Sam pulled into the driveway and grabbed a flashlight. A strong breeze flapped the cloth of the neighbor's American flag, and Sam could see the silhouette of tall pine trees swaying back and forth in the undeveloped woods behind the houses. A storm was rolling in.

Illuminating his path with a flashlight, Sam tried his luck with the front door but wasn't surprised to find it locked. Still, it was worth a shot. *Always try the easy way first*, he thought to himself.

Sam pulled a pick from his wallet. Aside from learning how to fight, picking a lock was probably the most important thing he learned while growing up in the foster care system. How far is a stable childhood going to get you when you're locked out of your house?

With two slight twists of his wrist, the doorknob clicked and opened easily. Sam was immediately hit by the bizarre combination of stale smoke and damp mold. He surveyed the disaster, which seemed even more foreboding in the dark.

Having already looked around upstairs, Sam stepped over debris as he walked through the first floor trying to re-imagine the crime. The back door had been unlocked, so it was possible that's how the assailant entered the house. Maybe Joe hadn't let his assailant in the front door after all.

So, assuming the killer came in through the back door, he must have snuck up the stairs and found Joe in his room. The fire had made it tough to check for blood in the bedroom, but they hadn't found blood anywhere else, which likely meant the assault was isolated to the one room.

The killer then lifted the body onto the bed and lit it up. He probably watched to make sure the fire took, then slipped out the back door.

Sam fumbled through the kitchen to find the door to the garage. You could learn a lot about a man by his garage.

When Sam opened the door, he was surprised to find the garage in immaculate condition. Silver shelves on every wall, filled with neatly arranged bins, garden accessories, winter gear and football pads. Along the wall that faced the automatic garage door was a long workbench made out of plywood and backed by a dark brown pegboard that held a variety of tools. A large gray Ford F-150 pickup truck sat in the middle of the garage.

Sam climbed up into the cabin and caught the new car smell. So, he hadn't had the truck long. The inside was clean and tidy, the glove compartment was empty—except for a pocket folder that held the registration and proof of insurance.

Sam hopped up into the pristine bed of the truck, opened the toolbox and half-heartedly shuffled through the collection of screwdrivers, wrenches and hammers. Nothing out of the ordinary.

Looking around, Sam studied the workbench. Everything seemed meticulously cared for—a far cry from the chaos of the rest of the house. From the vantage point of the back of the truck, he could see that every tool, every piece of wood, every box was arranged in order of descending height. All except one item—a large black coffee can. It stood out like a sore thumb.

Sam jumped down from the truck bed to get a better look. It was a solid black coffee can with a red diamond logo in the center that read Red Diamond Gourmet Coffee.

Sam was aware of the brand. He used to be a bit of a coffee fiend and had gotten to know many different labels. Red Diamond was a small coffee company out of Portland. They didn't distribute nationally, meaning you couldn't find it at the grocery store. The only way to get it was in Portland or through online orders.

Sam set the flashlight on the bench and picked up the can, expecting it to be heavy with random nails or screws. But it was so light it felt empty. Intrigued, he peeled back the plastic lid.

33

Sam pulled a pair of disposable latex gloves from his jacket pocket and slipped them on to help protect the potential evidence. He tipped the coffee can and poured out a pile of postcards. He picked one up. JOE REDDINGTON was scrawled in black Sharpie on one side. But there was no address and no stamp. He turned it over, heart pounding as he read the message:

YOU'RE GOING TO GET WHAT'S COMING TO YOU

It was signed with a single letter: M

Sam picked up another one. It carried another Sharpie-written note:

I CAN'T WAIT TO SEE YOU BURN – M

Another one read:

I'M GOING TO WATCH YOU DIE – M

There were at least two dozen of them. All handwritten notes. All signed by M.

34

Sam grabbed his bottle of beer and sat down at the small wooden table pushed into the corner of the living room.

His tiny one-bedroom was about one cockroach away from being condemned. A single 20x20 room served as kitchen, dining and living room. The white paint on the walls was chipped off in some places, while other areas were covered in deep yellow stains that Sam had always been afraid to investigate, much less clean. Two doors led to the rest of the apartment: a small bathroom and a tiny bedroom barely big enough for Sam's old twin-size mattress.

Aside from being run down, the apartment was also a mess. Clothes were scattered across the bedroom floor and much of the living room. The sink was full of dirty dishes and the trash can overflowed with paper plates and fast-food containers.

He took a swig from his beer as he opened the photos on his phone and scrolled through the pictures he had taken of all the postcards found at the Reddington house. Sam took the pictures before everything had been bagged. He laughed to himself. He couldn't remember the last time he had brought work home—unless it was some weed he had confiscated.

None of the postcards had a postmark, which meant they weren't sent through the mail. Joe had received them some another way. On the windshield of his car? At work? At home? Had Francine hid them?

Sam's phone began to vibrate and he was happy to see that the caller was Carla. He picked it up, trying to stifle his excitement and surprise.

"So, you couldn't get enough of me, huh?" he said with false bravado.

"Just curious if you found anything at the house," she answered, ignoring his question.

Sam told her about the coffee can full of postcards and read a few of them to her.

"The handwriting's consistent on all them," he said. "Big, bold letters scrawled with a black Sharpie."

"Any clue who wrote them?" Carla asked.

"I don't know. Can you think of any suspects with a letter M in their name?" he answered sarcastically.

35

The next morning, Sam drove toward the station to update Kaster on the case before paying Manny Rodriguez another visit. He didn't want to surprise his number one suspect too early, but if he waited too late, he risked finding him drunk again.

Thank goodness Carla had pushed him to go back to the scene of the crime. The notes would have gone unnoticed for who knows how long. Now, they were as close as Sam was probably going to get to a smoking gun. They wouldn't be enough to nab a conviction, but they could force a confession, which was what Sam was hoping to get from Rodriguez.

Sam's thoughts drifted to Carla and the kiss they shared the night before. He hadn't felt this way about anyone in years. Possibly decades. He needed to keep his nose clean. He couldn't blow this like he had blown everything else. This could be the fresh start he needed. The little bit of good luck that could turn his life around.

Sam was lost in his thoughts when something caught his eye. He was approaching a gas station on the edge of downtown and noticed someone milling around by the dumpsters. He squinted at the figure then quickly turned into the gas station.

"Doing a little afternoon dumpster diving?" Sam yelled as he got out of his car. The person spun around in surprise.

Yep. It was Mitch Reddington. He was wearing a gray T-shirt and blue track pants, both drenched with sweat. Mitch's hair was soaking wet, too. It looked like he'd been working out. But by a dumpster?

He seemed startled to see Sam. Like he got caught doing something wrong.

"I was just..." Mitch fumbled with an excuse but stopped when he finally recognized the cop. "Detective Lawson?"

Sam noticed Mitch's eyes darting back and forth on the ground, as if he was looking for something.

"You lose your contacts?" Sam asked. He could tell that Mitch didn't want his company.

Mitch told him he had gone for an afternoon run and saw some sort of animal back by the dumpster. A raccoon or possum or something. Sam was pretty sure Mitch was lying. Then again, he couldn't remember ever telling the truth to an adult—even when he hadn't done anything bad. Which, admittedly, was rare.

Knowing he was just given the opportunity to spend some one-on-one time with another M on his list, Sam decided to take his time with Mitch. He first asked about football to warm him up, and the subject did seem to spark him up a little. Mitch talked about the season and how the coach thought he had a shot at a scholarship. He told Sam how he was going to jump back in it. Sam nodded.

"Staying busy is probably a good thing," Sam said. "No sense just sitting around, right?"

Mitch seemed relieved that Sam understood. And when Sam asked him about the upcoming game, he got even more animated.

Despite his best efforts to stay removed and professional, Sam was soon wrapped up in it. He remembered seeing pictures of his own son playing football. It was one of his greatest regrets—not being there to see his son play. He always wondered what it would have been like to be in the stands, cheering him on. Pointing him out proudly to the other parents.

Sam asked Mitch if his dad had liked watching him play, and the way the smile on Mitch's face dropped made him immediately regret the question.

"Sorry," Sam said. "That was stupid of me."

"He came to every game," Mitch ignored Sam's apology. "I could hear him yelling in the stands louder than anyone."

"Your biggest fan, huh?" Sam said with a smile.

"He'd yell things like 'Hey, moron! Get your head in the game!' Or 'Stop playing like a little girl!'"

Sam wasn't sure what to say. He went with the obvious.

"Your dad sounds like a real dick."

That got a smirk out of Mitch. "I know it's wrong to say it, but I don't miss him," he answered.

Sam nodded. He had a feeling that getting taunted at football games wasn't the only reason Mitch didn't care for his dad.

Mitch started to say something else but stopped himself, struggling for the right words.

"It's bizarre not having him around," he finally said. "I know this sounds weird, but I think it's better."

"Your mom feel the same way?" Sam asked.

Mitch shrugged and kicked the ground. "She will."

Sam figured this was as good an opportunity as he was going to get, so he blurted out another question.

"Did your dad ever..." He struggled for the words. "Did he ever hurt you? On purpose?"

Sam could tell Mitch was studying him. Shit. It was one too many questions. Now Mitch was trying to decide if Sam was just curious or if he was interrogating him. Sam could see the caution in the young man's eyes slowly fill with anger.

"I can take care of myself," he finally grumbled through clenched teeth.

Then he told Sam he needed to finish his run and took off.

"You ever want to talk, you know where to find me," Sam yelled.

36

Warden Stivek used a strip of bacon to wipe up some of the runny yellow yolk still left on his plate. He washed it down with a sip of hot coffee, while half paying attention to the small TV that sat on the edge of the kitchen counter.

Local reporter Nancy Hellard was in the middle of a fluff piece about a local donkey that brayed at passing cars every morning. She was interviewing the donkey's owner when Marlene Stivek walked into the kitchen and poured herself a cup of coffee.

"Are they doing a report on that damn donkey again?" she asked her husband, half amused.

Marlene wore her shoulder length, bleached blonde hair big—in a style right out of the mid-eighties. It was the first thing you noticed about her. The second being her unfortunate spray tan. And, while she tended to wear more makeup than she needed to, she at least knew how to apply it so she didn't look like a clown.

She gave her husband a peck on the forehead and he wiped away the lipstick mark without even thinking about it.

"You look pretty," Warden Stivek said. "Anything special going on?"

Marlene looked down at her floral blouse and straightened the sleeves.

"I've got some grocery shopping to do," she said. "Lord knows who I'll see there, though. Always have to be prepared."

Stivek chuckled at his wife's vanity. He started to tease her, but his cell phone rang. It was Jeffery Hastings, his assistant.

"I ain't late for a meeting, am I?" he asked, only half seriously.

"Warden, it's about Manny Rodriguez."

The warden felt the blood drain from his face. He stood and quickly walked out of the kitchen and into the den, shutting the door behind him.

"What about him?" he finally asked.

"He's back in town. Has been for a while," Hastings said.

"For a while?" Stivek blurted. "Why am I just now finding out about this?"

Hastings stuttered and stammered with his response. "I just found out myself."

Stivek couldn't believe the ex-con had the nerve to come back to town after he had made it crystal clear what would happen to him if he showed his face again.

"It gets worse," Hastings finally said. "The cops have already talked to him."

Stivek felt his stomach do a nose dive as Hastings continued. He told him that Lawson had paid Rodriguez a visit a couple of days earlier.

"Lawson? That cocky son of a bitch who came to the prison?"

Stivek scratched at his thick mustache and looked at the deer heads mounted on the wood-paneled walls.

"Did he say anything?" he finally asked.

Hastings told him that he wasn't sure, but he knew that he wasn't brought into the police station.

"Either he didn't say enough or Lawson didn't believe him," Stivek muttered to himself.

He ordered Hastings to see what else he could find out, then quickly hung up. He looked out the window at two squirrels chasing each other up a tree. He wished he could have kept Rodriguez in prison, where he would have been able to keep a proper eye on him. But, as usual, the damn Parole Board decided they knew better. He wondered if they were regretting their decision now.

He began plotting and calculating, going over possible scenarios in his head, and he quickly formulated a plan. He would need to call Police Chief Kaster and see if he could call off that Lawson detective. But first, he needed to make another call. It was time to nip this Manny Rodriguez problem in the bud.

37

Mitch tensed his entire body as the burn slowly seared through his skin. He gritted his teeth and tried not to yell. The pain was intense and concentrated and he began to feel light-headed. Finally, after what seemed like an eternity, it began to fade, soon to be replaced with a different pain. A steady, throbbing burn that seemed to spread up his leg.

He opened his eyes and only then realized how tight he had been gripping the edge of his chair.

"You ever gonna talk back to me like that again?" his father asked, holding the cigarette in front of him as if to dare him to answer yes.

Mitch shook his head.

"I can't hear you," his father said slowly.

Mitch could barely talk through the pain. "No, sir."

"What was that?" his father yelled.

"No, sir!" Mitch yelled.

He felt a tear trickle down his cheek and he hoped his father didn't see it. He let it roll slowly, knowing he couldn't draw attention to it by wiping it away.

His father took one last drag off the cigarette before flicking it into *the kitchen sink. He pushed away the kitchen chair as he stood, towering over his son.*

"Now get outta here," he sneered.

Mitch rolled his blue jeans down, being careful not to touch the fresh cigarette burn on his ankle. The welt was a deep red, the only thing setting it apart from all the other burns on his leg.

38

"So, you think the cops are going to ask me?" Caleb said, snapping Mitch back to reality. He absent-mindedly reached down to rub the old wounds around his ankle.

Mitch took the silver vape pen from his friend and took a long draw on it, holding his breath to let the marijuana absorb into his lungs.

He leaned his head back and felt the numbness roll down his body. It was the first time he had relaxed since the fire.

Caleb McConnell took the vape pen back and inhaled deeply. Caleb was tall and lean with fair skin and white blonde hair. Other than the acne that peppered his cheeks and the nose he hadn't quite grown into yet, he looked much older than his seventeen years.

He and Mitch had been friends since fourth grade and were more like brothers. They had been there for each other through just about everything—from the divorce of Caleb's parents to winning the district championship last football season. And, of course, through the rocky terrain that was Mitch's relationship with his father.

Even though they were almost too big for it, they still hung out in the same tree house they had built in the woods when they were in middle school. It was nothing more than a triangle-shaped landing made of six two-by-fours nailed to two tree branches that jutted out from a tall pine in the woods behind Caleb's property. They had nailed smaller planks into the tree to create ladder rungs up to their lookout. It had seemed so high when they had first built it. Now it was just slightly taller than either of them.

"I don't know," Mitch finally answered. "Probably not. But just in case."

"Okay," Caleb answered. Then he laughed. "Never thought I'd have to lie about NOT ditching practice."

Mitch laughed, too. It was true. They were constantly ditching practice. Mitch was surprised Coach let them get away with it but a) they were both too good of players and b) the team was so small there weren't enough backups to fill in for them.

"Remember that time we ran out to your car right in the middle of practice, smoked a bowl, then came right back before Coach even saw we were gone?" Caleb said, still laughing.

They both started snickering, only partly due to the effects of the vape pen. The laughter finally waned, and the two sat in a comfortable silence again.

"I can't wait until things get back to normal," Mitch finally said.

"Is it going to be weird?" Caleb asked. "Not having him around?"

Mitch took another drag. "The sooner I can forget him the better."

"My mom told me the funeral is Saturday," Caleb said, his voice growing quiet. "That's gonna suck."

Mitch sighed. He was dreading the funeral. Having to pretend he's sad. Having to listen to everyone talk about how deep down, he was a good man. It turned his stomach.

"Maybe we can skip out of that, too," Caleb offered.

Mitch liked the idea but knew he couldn't. He needed to be there for his mom. She would need him that day. For reasons he could never understand, she loved his father.

"Or maybe after," Caleb continued. "Aren't they having a reception at your aunt's house? She lives by the lake, right? They got a boat?"

Mitch nodded. "We can't take the big boat, but even going out on the rowboat would be fun."

"It'd be better than sitting around eating crappy food with a bunch of hypocrites," Caleb said, snorting.

He was right, thought Mitch. They were all hypocrites. His dad was an asshole and everyone knew it. The world was better off without him, and he hated that he had to get dressed up and pretend otherwise.

"So, were you able to save any of your stuff from the house?" Caleb asked, switching gears.

"Not really," Mitch answered matter-of-factly.

"That sucks."

Mitch shrugged. "Nothing there but bad memories anyway."

"So, did you get to see the fire at all?" Caleb finally asked. "Was it still burning when you got there?"

Mitch told him what he remembered, which wasn't much. When he and his mother arrived, they had both sat in the car in shock, unable to believe that the house in front of them was their own. The fire had already been put out, but smoke was still pouring from the upstairs—especially the open wall to what used to be his parents' bedroom.

They had both gotten out of the car and just stared. Then his mom started calling out for his dad. When they couldn't find him anywhere, the shock turned to panic. His mom began screaming and running toward the house. Mitch didn't remember much after that. Everything was a blur.

"Remember the little fires we used to set in the woods?" Caleb asked with a chuckle. "Man, it's a wonder we didn't burn the town down."

Mitch remembered. They would make piles of dried pine needles and use a magnifying glass to concentrate the heat from the sun. He still remembered the tiny bright light the magnifying glass would make. How the needles would start smoking and then glowing red, shrinking and recoiling under the heat. Then, suddenly a flame would rise up, appearing like a magic trick. They would pile more pine needles on top of the flame, letting the fire grow. Then, before it could get out of hand, they would smother it in dirt.

"What about the... you know?" Caleb spoke more quietly, even though no one could hear them.

Mitch thought about the box he had managed to sneak out. He had hidden it under some large rocks behind some dumpsters and had gone back there this morning to retrieve it. Unfortunately, he had been interrupted by that weird detective. He had to jog off then, but he came back later.

"I got it," he answered.

Caleb sat back in relief. "Thank God."

"I hid it at my aunt's house," he said. "It's safe."

39

Sam decided small talk wasn't a good idea with an impatient Rodriguez. The ex-con had let Sam in without any problem, almost as if he'd been expecting him. Sam sat down and asked Rodriguez if he'd been anywhere or seen anyone. The answer didn't surprise him. Rodriguez hadn't left his couch since they last spoke. The empty bottles and cans of beer littered all around the sofa seemed to corroborate his story.

"Look, you're a busy man so I won't waste too much of your time," Sam said, pulling out his phone. He pulled up the pictures he had taken of the threatening postcards and showed them to Rodriguez.

"Did you write these?"

Rodriguez stared at the phone.

"What are they?" he asked calmly.

"Did you write them?" Sam asked again.

Rodriguez took another swig of tequila. "Do I look like I write letters?"

Sam pointed out the M signatory that went with each threat.

"Know anyone with a name that starts with the letter M?" Sam asked sarcastically. "Come on, man. Talk to me."

He could see the anger building in Rodriguez.

"I told you already. I didn't kill him. Death was too good for that son of a bitch," Rodriguez grumbled behind gritted teeth.

Sam decided to dig a little deeper this time.

"What did he do to you?" he asked.

Rodriguez stared into Sam's eyes for an uncomfortably long time. Finally, he scrounged around through some of the clutter on the floor. He pulled up a small framed photo and handed it to Sam. The picture was old—probably ten years or so. It was a wedding photo of a fresh-faced Rodriguez and a beautiful Mexican woman.

"That's Maria."

Rodriguez's tattoo.

Sam looked at the handsome couple. All smiles and happiness.

"She's beautiful, isn't she?" Rodriguez asked with a sad gentleness in his voice.

"When I got sent here, she moved to town so she could be close to me. Did housekeeping at a motel. Visited me every chance she got."

He drank down more tequila. Sam noticed the bottle was almost empty.

"What he did to her..."

Sam saw the rage start to build inside the ex-con. Now red in the face, Rodriguez let out a primal yell and hurled the tequila bottle across the room. It hit the edge of a cabinet and shattered into a million pieces.

Sam froze in place, ready to jump to his escape if Rodriguez decided to take his anger out on him. But instead, the ex-con fell back into the couch, the burst of anger had drained him of all energy.

"That shit bag deserved to die," Rodriguez finally growled under his breath.

Sam was afraid to ask the obvious question but he knew he had to.

"What did Joe do to her?"

Rodriguez shook his head and looked down, as if he had to build up strength just to answer the question.

"When she showed up to see me," he finally said. "He would find ways to keep me away. Throw me in solitary on some bogus shit. Tell her I didn't want to see her. Whatever. Then he'd..."

He pointed to the grocery bag that Sam had brought in with him. Sam pulled out a six-pack of beer—his backup—and handed it to Rodriguez, who opened one and gulped almost all of it down.

"He made her meet him at the motel where she worked."

Sam felt his stomach turn.

"Then he'd tell her he'd find ways to keep me inside forever if she didn't cooperate," he said. Sam could hear the rage in his quivering voice.

Sam was stunned. He knew Joe was an asshole, but this took it to a new level.

"What about other guards?" Sam asked. "They had to have seen him."

Rodriguez shook his head. "They knew. They all knew."

"Where is she now?" Sam finally asked, afraid of the answer.

Rodriguez looked up at him, is eyes red with tears and fury.

"I think she's dead."

40

Sam took a swig of whiskey from the bottle. If he was going to have to spend his evening sitting in his car, he was going to at least enjoy it.

The whiskey burned as it slid down Sam's throat. It was a feeling he was used to—even enjoyed. Different liquor felt differently. Whiskey left a smoky, earthy burn that grounded Sam. Tequila's aftertaste, on the other hand, was lighter and sinister. In many ways, they were the yin and yang of Sam's preferred liquors. Whiskey was a perfect way to end a bad day, while tequila was a great way to start a wild night. Whiskey soothed his soul, while tequila woke up his demons. Of course, other spirits had their own identities. Vodka was colder and more chemical, but easier to take... and hide. And gin... well, gin was pretty much just flavored vodka. It always reminded Sam of Christmas trees. Maybe that's why he hated it so much.

He screwed the cap back on the bottle and set it in the plastic compartment between the seats. Too much of that would put him right to sleep and he had a long night in front of him. He reached over to the cardboard fast food container in the passenger seat and grabbed a handful of cold fries, dipping them in a pool of ketchup he had squirted onto a napkin before stuffing them all in his mouth at once.

Rodriguez's urge to talk dried up as soon as the booze did. Sam had thought about bringing him into the station to sober him up but was pretty sure Rodriguez would not go quietly, and Sam was in no shape to fight. Besides, Sam was responsible for getting him drunk—something that would not go over well with Kaster.

Instead, after making a quick trip to Whataburger to load up on meals for the night, he returned and pulled his car out of sight to keep an eye on things. He doubted Rodriguez posed any kind of flight risk—the man could barely even stand up. But he might have an accomplice. Sam could gather information just as easily from his car while also keeping an eye on Rodriguez.

He parked at the edge of the trailer park. It was far enough away and hidden behind a cluster of trees to not rouse suspicion of the other trailer parkers, but still close enough that he could see Rodriguez's humble abode. And there he sat. For the rest of the day and now into the night.

Sam took another bite of his burger. He looked at his watch. Only a little past nine. "Maybe I should have bought two burgers," he thought.

He couldn't stop thinking about everything the ex-con had said. With a few more beers and the right questions, Rodriguez had gone on to make some pretty serious accusations that could implicate a hell of a lot of people.

He told Sam that Reddington had made his wife meet him on multiple occasions at the motel, each time forcing himself on her. At the time, Rodriguez didn't know what was going on. Only that Maria had stopped visiting him. Then, out of the blue, she called him.

She told him everything. That she didn't know how to stop it, but she couldn't go on. Sam remembered how Rodriguez's voice had changed when he talked about the call. A gentleness had come over him and he barely spoke in a whisper.

Shortly after that, Rodriguez's parole review came up and, much to his surprise, it was granted. But before he left, Warden Stivek told him to get as far away from Quinton as possible. He told him that his wife had gone back to El Paso so Rodriguez headed there. But her family hadn't heard from her in months. He had just recently returned to Quinton in search for answers about her disappearance. He was convinced that Reddington had killed her and the warden had covered it up. Of course, he had no proof. And the accusations of a drunk ex-con had fallen on deaf ears.

Sam spent the evening making calls from his car to check out the story. There was no record of any dead bodies that matched Maria's description. And the prison visitation record showed that she had visited several times and then just stopped. Beyond that, there was nothing.

Sam had reluctantly left a message for Chief Kaster. He knew the chief was tight with Warden Stivek and probably would brush the whole thing off. But Sam decided to bet on the chief respecting the law over his friends. Maybe there was a chance the chief had information that could help the case.

Sam also left a message with Charlie Paloma. Maybe the guard could fill him in on what Rodriguez had been talking about. He had to have heard something. Maybe that was why he was so nervous about giving up Rodriguez's name.

Sam let out a long yawn. Even though the heat had tempered, the humidity was still oppressive and it covered him like a blanket. He couldn't run the car engine because it would attract attention, which meant he had no AC. He had opened the windows and prayed for a cross-breeze, but tonight the air was still. Sam listened to the chorus of frogs and crickets that sang to him like nature's lullaby. He leaned back in his seat. Maybe he would rest his eyes. Just for a second.

The loud noise woke Sam up with a start. Disoriented, he looked around and realized the whiskey bottle had fallen off its perch on to the floorboard covered in other empty bottles. He yawned and rubbed his eyes to get his bearings.

"How long had I dozed off?" he wondered. He looked at his watch and was shocked to see an hour had passed by.

Then he noticed something else. A glow coming from the direction of Rodriguez's trailer. As he became aware of the smell of smoke, he began to register what he was seeing.

"What the hell?" Sam said, as a jolt of panic shot through him.

He jumped out of his car and started running toward Rodriguez's trailer that was engulfed in flames.

41

The sun was just peeking through the trees and the trailer was all but gone. Nothing was left but charred remains of metal, plastic and burnt wood. The walls to the trailer had melted or fallen, so there was no door to walk through. It looked like a bomb had hit it.

By the time Sam woke up, the trailer was so engulfed in flames there was no way he could have gotten inside to save Rodriguez. Firefighters arrived shortly after, but it was too late to salvage anything. Now, hours later, the area was surrounded by police cars, fire trucks and a couple of news vans. Sam sat on the back of an ambulance while a paramedic stitched up a gash on his forehead he had received as he tried to get in the trailer.

As the paramedic finished up, Sam spotted the fire investigator, Tim Nieman, at the far end of the trailer remains, probably where the bedroom had been. Sam walked along the outer edge of the ashes.

"Anything?" he yelled to Nieman.

Nieman looked up and visibly groaned when he saw Sam. He stood and carefully walked through the black and gray dust to where Sam was standing.

"There's what's left of a body on what was probably the bed. Unrecognizable, but we'll check the DNA. Pretty sure it's Manny Rodriguez."

Sam's heart sank. He had hoped Rodriguez had snuck out of the trailer while he had been passed out.

Sam hadn't told anyone he had fallen asleep. His official story was that he was watching the house and noticed something that looked odd. By the time he realized it was fire, the trailer was engulfed. The rest of his story was true. He had tried to go in for Rodriguez, but the flames had forced him back and he could do nothing but watch helplessly while he waited for the fire department.

"Find anything? Any clues?" Sam asked.

"You were here. You saw how fast it went up," Nieman said, not hiding his disdain for the detective. "It's hard to get a clear read yet, but looks like some sort of accelerant was used in the bedroom. However, given the history of the victim, your guys aren't ready to call it a homicide yet."

Not ready to call it a homicide?

Sam turned around to where Nieman was looking. Kaster was talking to a couple of firefighters. Sam left Nieman without a word and walked up to his boss.

"You're ruling out homicide?" he asked loudly before he even reached his boss. Kaster looked up. Seeing Sam, he said something to the firefighters then walked toward the detective.

"We're not ruling it out, but, come on," Kaster said, "the guy clearly killed himself."

Kaster pointed in the direction of where Sam's car was still parked.

"You were sitting right up there," he said.

Sam nodded.

"Don't you think you would have seen something? Or someone? Or even heard something?" Kaster asked. "But the way you described it was, 'there was nothing and then suddenly something that looked like a flame and then the whole place went up.'"

Sam was getting buried by his own lie.

"Besides," Kaster added. "We found a note."

Sam tried to hide his surprise about a note, but it must have been obvious to the chief.

"Oh, you didn't know about that?" Kaster asked. "You mean you didn't get all the facts before you started jumping to conclusions?"

Sam ignored him. "Where is it?"

"It's bagged."

"What'd it say?" Sam asked, trying to keep his cool. The whole thing smelled like bullshit to him. Rodriguez was too drunk to write.

"Nothing surprising," Kaster said with a shrug. "Prayed God would forgive him. But Joe Reddington got what he deserved and he didn't regret killing him. Blah blah blah."

That sounded way more coherent than the Rodriguez Sam had talked to. The Rodriguez who had said he wasn't the letter writing type.

"Pretty much your standard confession," Kaster said grinning. "Makes your job easier. I'm sure you like that."

"Where did you even find the note?" Sam asked. "The whole place is gone."

Kaster pointed to the wooden post that served as the address marker.

"It was taped to that," Kaster said. "Signed, sealed, delivered."

42

"Come on, Chief," Sam said. "Don't you think I would have seen him put a note there?"

But Sam doubted himself. Could Rodriguez have slipped out and put the note on the post while Sam was checked out? Or even when he had run out for food?

Kaster shrugged. "He could have done it earlier. I don't know. I'm just glad we can put this all behind us now."

"Don't you think it's all just a little too neat and tidy?" Sam asked.

Kaster laughed. "Since when have you ever complained about that?" He patted Sam on the back. "Go home and rest. We'll take a fresh look after forensics gathers their data. But my guess is we can put a bow on this one."

Sam still wasn't ready to let it go.

"You got my voicemail, right?" Sam asked. "About what Rodriguez had said?"

Kaster laughed. "His conspiracy theory? Come on, Sam. You know better than that."

"We should at least check it out," Sam replied.

Kaster sighed. "We just went through this, Lawson. It's open and shut as it needs to be. Two assholes are dead. They cancel each other out. Family gets closure, and we can go on to solving crimes that matter."

"What about Rodriguez's wife?" Sam asked. "This could all be a cover-up."

"You've been watching too much TV," Kaster replied.

"You're just trying to protect your buddy Stivek," Sam heard himself saying.

Kaster's face went cold. "What the fuck did you just say?"

Don't say any more, Sam thought to himself. *This won't end well.*

"Nothing," he finally said. "I said nothing."

He turned to walk away, but Kaster yelled at him to stop. He turned and stared at his boss in disgust.

"If I even hear a rumor that you're bothering the Reddingtons or the warden or any of the guards, I will take your badge and shove it so far up your ass, your eyes will shine."

Sam took a step toward Kaster. "Thanks for the visual. You been practicing that one?"

Kaster stepped toward Sam. The two men were now chest to chest.

"I saw the bottle in your car and I can still smell the booze on your breath," Kaster growled. "If you'd like, I'd be happy to add that to my official report."

Sam took a step back.

"Go. Home. Now," Kaster said. His words were slow and deliberate.

"Even if Rodriguez did kill Reddington and then killed himself, don't you even want to know why?" Sam asked, knowing he was pushing his luck.

"Watch my lips," Kaster said. "No one cares."

Sam felt sick to his stomach. What was going on? He began to walk back to his car, confused by everything. A huge weight of guilt began to push down on him. Rodriguez was dead because Sam had dropped the ball. If he hadn't been drinking, he wouldn't have passed out. He would have seen the fire start and could have gotten Rodriguez out in time.

Sam was a lazy detective and a drunk. He thought about Carla. About his son. About the way the other cops always looked at him. Then he thought about the man he used to be. He was a total disappointment.

He sighed.

"No," he thought to himself. "Someone's gotta expect something from you before you can be a disappointment."

43

The cup of black coffee swirled in front of him as Sam stirred in the packet of sugar. He tossed back a handful of Tylenol then sipped the hot beverage to wash it down. Carla had asked to meet him here and he had barely had time to go home and wash the smoke out of his hair (and brush the booze from his breath).

He looked around the Lone Star Diner. Just a few booths and a counter with the kitchen behind it. There was an open window into the kitchen where the waitresses would place and pick up the orders. Sam could hear the sounds of country music coming from the other side of the window. He was always more of a rock 'n' roll guy, but the sad sounds of the steel guitar fit his mood perfectly.

Out of nowhere, Carla slid into the seat across from him, startling him out of his thoughts.

"What the fuck, Sam?" she practically shouted.

The words hit him like a brick.

"You could have gotten yourself killed," she said. He could feel the anger in her voice.

"I'm fine," Sam protested.

"What happened?" she asked.

The next thing he knew, everything was spilling out. He told her everything that Rodriguez had told him. About his wife's visit. The accusations of rape. Covering up her death.

"And you didn't see anyone around the trailer?" she asked.

Sam looked down as he shook his head again. "I may have turned my head. For just a second. But you know how those trailer fires are. They go up in seconds."

Carla stared at him as if waiting for him to say something else. Finally, she broke her silence.

"You were drinking, weren't you?" she asked. But it was more of a statement than a question.

Sam started to argue but he had no lies left in him.

"You passed out in your car, didn't you?" She asked, clearly aware of the answer. "You don't know what happened because you were passed out. Holy shit."

Sam wanted to defend himself. He hadn't passed out. He just fell asleep. Granted, the alcohol in his system didn't help things. But he certainly didn't pass out. But he knew she wouldn't believe him. He had earned her judgement and he wanted to crawl under a rock.

"If you don't get yourself killed, you're gonna get yourself fired," she continued. "Is that what you want?"

Sam shook his head.

"All day long, I deal with dead people. You know what they all have in common?" she asked. "They didn't think they were going to die. They all thought they had more time."

They were interrupted by Nora, their waitress. She topped off Sam's coffee and poured a cup for Carla without even asking.

Nora had been working at the Lone Star for most of her fifty-year life. She was thin as a rail and wore an ill-fitting auburn wig. Her bright blue eyes had dulled over the years and her weathered skin made her look older than she really was.

"Y'all working on the murder?" she asked. "The guy that got burnt up?"

Sam noticed the wrinkles around her lips—the kind you earn from a lifetime of smoking cigarettes.

"Makes my skin crawl knowing there's a killer out there," she said before walking back to the kitchen.

Sam and Carla sat in silence for a few minutes.

"So what are you going to do now?" Carla asked. She had calmed down.

Sam shrugged. "I don't know what I can do."

"I heard the official story. What do you think happened?" Carla asked.

He took the fact she wanted to talk about the case as a good sign. Maybe she hadn't given up on him yet.

"According to Rodriguez, Joe Reddington raped his wife to the point that she killed herself. Then the warden covered up her death. I think he needed to make sure Reddington would keep quiet, so he unleashed Rodriguez on him. That makes Rodriguez the only loose end. And now suddenly he's dead, too."

He studied Carla's face, trying to determine if she thought he was completely crazy.

"My judgement may not always be great, but my instincts are," he said.

She finally nodded and took one last sip of coffee before standing up.

"I'll see what I can dig up. In the meantime, you need to get your shit together," she said. "It's not cute."

He sat in silence and watched her walk out of the diner. He knew she was right. He also knew he needed to talk to Charlie Paloma.

44

Charlie peeked through the slats of his window blinds. Nervous sweat beaded on his forehead as he saw Sam's Plymouth pull into the driveway. He was at the door before the detective could even knock, practically pulling him inside.

"Jesus, what are you doing here?" Charlie asked.

"We need to talk," Sam answered.

Sam told Charlie about the fire at Rodriguez's trailer. How they were trying to sell it to look like suicide. But Sam wasn't buying. Charlie started to freak out.

"You have to protect me," Charlie said. "This is way more than I bargained for."

"Whoa. Slow down," Sam replied. "Protect you from who?"

"From *them*," Charlie said, clearly annoyed that Sam wasn't keeping up. "They must know I talked to you. Shit. Shit. Shit."

He paced the room, pausing to peek through the blinds again.

"They. Them," Sam mocked. "I'm going to need more than that, Charlie."

"The warden," Charlie said, exasperated. "And his cronies."

"He's got cronies?" Sam asked.

"A couple of other guards. You don't think he gets his own hands dirty, do you?"

"I need names," Sam said.

"Did you talk to Rodriguez?" Charlie asked.

Sam told Charlie everything Rodriguez had told him. The accusations against Joe and his belief they had killed his wife. Charlie listened but kept shaking his head, like he didn't want to hear it.

"So is it true?" Sam finally asked.

Charlie said he didn't know, but Sam wasn't buying it. Finally, Charlie relented.

"Joe had done it before. With other prisoner's wives," Charlie said. "He'd take advantage of them a few times then move on to someone else. But Rodriguez's wife... "

"Maria," Sam interjected. "Her name was Maria."

Charlie nodded.

"What I heard is that Joe went to the motel where she worked. That's where he would... you know. And he found her. Dead. She'd hung herself. He called the warden, and they took care of the body and covered it all up."

"Then Rodriguez kills Reddington and the warden has Rodriguez killed," Sam said.

Charlie started pacing the room nervously.

"What if they know I know?" Charlie asked. "They'll come after me next. I should have kept my big mouth shut."

Sam was too busy piecing everything together to listen to Charlie. It all made sense except, for some reason, he still had a hard time believing Rodriguez killed Reddington. He was too much of a drunk. He didn't have a car. If the warden wanted Joe dead, he wouldn't have entrusted that job to a drunk.

"You've got to stop them, Detective," Charlie said.

Sam stood up, telling Charlie to sit tight.

"What are you going to do?" Charlie asked.

Sam smiled. "I need to find the warden."

45

Sam used to joke that the perfect time to go on a robbery spree in Quinton would be Friday night because that's when everyone was at the high school football game.

That's why Sam knew he'd be able to find Warden Stivek there.

He'd spent the entire day trying to chase the warden down. He couldn't find him at the prison and he hadn't been at his home either. Luckily, it was Friday night so there was one more place to look. The football game.

High school football was as much an aural experience as a visual one. The sound of the drums in the high school band banged out a staccato rhythm complemented by an occasional cymbal crash. The cheerleaders, who stood on the sidelines, yelled a chant in unison and the crowd cheered back on cue. It was all punctuated by shrill whistles from the referees and coaches barking plays at the team from the sideline.

Sam stood at the bottom of the stands, facing the crowd. He scoured the sea of faces. As usual, the stands were packed with students, parents and just about everyone else in town. Finally, he spotted his target. Warden Stivek, dressed in a bright blue golf shirt that matched the team's colors. He sat next to a blonde with an obnoxiously fake tan. Exactly the type of woman Sam would expect him to be married to.

Sam moved into the warden's line of vision until he got his attention. The warden unconsciously stiffened and Sam enjoyed seeing the nervousness in his eyes. He motioned for Stivek to follow him, then walked away from the crowds and toward the entry gate. As he walked out of view, he pressed the Record button on his phone.

It didn't take long for Stivek to catch up to Sam, and the two men stepped off of the path, to the side of the concession stand. In one swift movement, Sam grabbed Stivek by his shirt collar and slammed him into the side of the building.

"I know you're involved with all of this," Sam said.

Stivek pushed Sam away and straightened his shirt.

"You must have really had your brain rattled, Detective," Stivek said. "You are about to enter a world of hurt."

"Cut the bullshit. I know everything," Sam snapped.

The warden stared at him. Sam saw a glimpse of fear in his eyes. Sam hated men like Stivek. He was a chicken shit who acted tough but never got his own hands dirty. He was also powerful, and Sam realized he had made a mistake manhandling him. But it was too late now. Sam had nothing to lose so he went for it.

"Joe Reddington raped Maria Rodriguez on your watch—to the point where she killed herself," he said. "And when Reddington asked you for help, you knew you couldn't have that kind of scandal come out."

"I don't know what you're talking about," the warden insisted.

Sam spelled it out for him. How the warden covered up

Maria's death. How he got rid of Joe when he realized he couldn't keep his mouth shut.

"But you needed a scapegoat," he continued. "Luckily, Manny Rodriguez was up for parole, so all you had to do was let him out and frame him for your dirty work. But then I got to Rodriguez, and you got worried he would talk. You couldn't have that."

"So, I killed him?" Stivek shot back, pushing Sam away. "Use what little brain cells you have left, son. If what you say had really happened, with this woman... whatever her name was. If all that were true, were people talking about it? Was there a scandal? No. So why would I go and start killing people and draw attention to it?"

That actually made sense, Sam thought.

"Joe Reddington's murder would have been the last thing I would have wanted. That would only attract attention," Stivek said, jutting his finger in Sam's face.

Sam couldn't even think of a smart-ass comeback.

"And, by the way, who the fuck even cares?" Stivek said. "If you're even half a detective, you'd know by now that Joe Reddington was no one worth crying over and neither was Manny Rodriguez."

Sam thought about it all, letting it sink in.

"Now if you'll excuse me, I'm missing the game," Stivek said, walking past Sam and yelling back over his shoulder.

"Stay out of the deep end, son," Stivek said. "You don't look like that strong of a swimmer."

Sam watched him walk away, stunned. This did NOT go as he had planned. As he walked back to his car, he thought about what Stivek had said. It all made sense. But what about Rodriguez? Why would he make up such a story? Stivek had to be lying. But Kaster had tied his hands, so there was no way he could keep digging.

Sam had an idea. He might not be able to investigate the

warden any further, but that doesn't mean someone else couldn't.

He pulled out his phone and dialed. A voice on the other end answered.

"Nancy Hellard."

46

Sam took a long draw of cold beer from the bottle, eyeing all the colorful liquor bottles behind the bar. If he ever needed a drink, it was tonight.

He pulled his cell phone from his pocket to check the time. 8:13. He had asked her to meet him at 8.

Maybe Stivek was telling the truth. Maybe he wasn't part of a murderous cover-up. Maybe one bastard had just killed another bastard and that was it. But there was still the issue of what had happened to Rodriguez's wife. If Sam wasn't allowed to look into it, and his own boss refused to do it, then the least he could do was point an ambitious reporter in the right direction. What's the worst that could come of it? Stivek gets publicly shamed a little? Kaster gets mud on his face for playing politics? Sam smiled. He could live with that.

Nancy Hellard apologized for running late. They weren't used to this much crime in Quinton. First a murder/fire and then the murderer is killed in a suicide/fire?

"Please tell me you've got more to this story," she said.

Sam smiled. Boy, did he. He told her everything he knew, and she hungrily wrote it all down. He told her about the notes in the coffee can and even shared the pictures of the notes that he had taken. He told her about meeting Rodriguez and his claims about Joe Reddington. He told her about the rumored suicide of Maria Rodriquez and potential cover-up by the warden.

Nancy was practically drooling as she scribbled down her notes. She was thrilled with the information and said it corroborated other rumors she had uncovered. That made Sam feel better.

"I have one request," he said to her. "I need to remain anonymous."

"You'd be a questionable source anyway," she replied. "But I need more than rumors from an anonymous source. I need something concrete."

Sam thought for a second.

"I may have a source for you," he said. "If I can talk him into it."

47

Carla slid the remains of Manny Rodriguez back into the cooler drawer. Two charred bodies in one week was a new record for her and not one she was looking forward to breaking any time soon. Her initial examination supported Kaster's claim of suicide. There was no sign of another injury, like there had been with Joe Reddington. And the cause of Rodriguez's death was definitely smoke inhalation. He also had a blood alcohol level of 2.1. So it was possible he was already passed out when the fire started. But there was no way she could prove that.

She decided to wait to call Sam with the news. Maybe she could find something else for him. She wondered if she was doing the right thing. Was he just the washed-up drunk everyone said he was? Carla didn't want to believe it. In fact, she had convinced herself otherwise. But then he pulled the incident at the trailer park. It was not a good sign.

Maybe he just had a slip up. Maybe he just needed a little support. Someone to believe in him. Still, she was not in the market for a fixer-upper. However, regardless of her conflicted feelings about Sam, she was definitely enjoying the detective work. She loved her job but there weren't a lot of murders in

Quinton. And the two bodies she had in her cooler were so badly burned that she couldn't get much more from them than she already had.

She rolled her chair across the concrete floor to the old metal desk situated in the corner. Her office, as it were.

48

Carla's eyes never left the screen as she dipped a baby carrot into a plastic container of hummus. She had been looking up everything she could on Manny Rodriguez and his wife, Maria. But there was nothing out of the ordinary. And her research on Joe Reddington didn't fare much better.

There were a few old newspaper articles online from his high school days. He had led his baseball team to a conference championship and he was quite the star. But he never went to college. Probably because of no scholarships, which was probably because of his arrest record. At seventeen, he was charged with aggravated assault and spent six months in juvenile detention. After that, the criminal record amped up. One breaking and entering—but no robbery. A couple of drunk and disorderlies. But after high school, he seemed to clean up. Much to Carla's surprise, there were no domestic disturbances. Sam had told her about the scuffles at football games, but they turned out to be nothing too serious and no charges were ever brought against him.

She wondered how far the apple had fallen from the tree and had started digging up info on Mitch Reddington, as well.

There were no police records but she was able to get her hands on some school files, where she found Mitch had been involved in quite a few altercations. The phrase "anger issues" came up a lot.

It was enough to make her want to learn more about the Reddington family. She looked at the cardboard box of material she had gathered at the public library. Carla had pulled a favor from a librarian friend. Normally, she wouldn't have been able to take the assortment of old newspapers and high school yearbooks out of the library, but her friend had made an exception. It didn't hurt that Carla worked for the police department.

She pulled out a yearbook. Its white cover was frayed at the binding and it was covered in scuff marks and water stains. She flipped through the pages, looking for Joe's senior picture. She had seen recent pictures in the newspaper articles about his murder. He actually hadn't changed that much. A little rougher around the edges. A little heavier. But that was about it.

She flipped through the pages to the sports section. There he was again, standing front and center of the baseball team. She flipped through other pages, looking for Francine's picture. She was Francine Travis then.

Unlike Joe's picture, Francine looked very different. She had aged a lot. But, from what Sam had told Carla, she could understand why. She was such a pretty young woman then. There was a sparkle in her eye that had long since fizzled out. She was young and filled with hope and promise.

Carla thought about her own senior year. If you would have told her then that she'd be a county medical examiner—working with dead people all day long—young Carla would have laughed you out of the room. She was going to be a biologist. Or maybe a psychologist. Thinking back, she couldn't really tell you when her path started veering away from her youthful dreams. That's how the path of least resistance works, she thought. Next thing you know, you're sitting in the dark with a bunch of dead bodies looking at a stranger's old yearbook.

She wondered what Sam had been like in high school. Probably not much different, she thought with a smile. Immature, impulsive, but charming as hell. Probably got away with murder with just a smile.

She thought about their conversation this morning at the diner. She felt bad that she was so hard on him, but he needed to hear it. And, to be honest, he had scared her. When she had heard he had been hurt, it sent a jolt of panic through her. She realized she cared for him. But she was not going to fall for another man-child.

As she let the pages of the yearbook fan past her, something caught her attention. Was that another picture of Francine? She leafed back through the pages until she found it. When she saw the picture, she gasped out loud.

49

After the game, Caleb had dropped Mitch off in front of his aunt's lake house. But instead of going right inside, Mitch took the opportunity to head to the storage shed out back and check on the box he had retrieved from behind the convenience store. He knew it was safe. He would have definitely heard about it if someone had discovered it. But still, he wanted to be sure.

He grabbed the flashlight off the shelf and clicked it on, navigating his way through the lawn tools and around the riding lawnmower to get to a cabinet in back. He got down on all fours and reached into a small space at the back of the cabinet until he was able to grab the small box. He inched it out with his fingers until he could get a better grip, then he pulled it all the way out.

Mitch took the box to the riding lawnmower, where he sat down, opened it and pulled out a handgun.

A revolver, to be more exact. Mitch checked the chambers. It was still loaded. Still ready if he ever needed it.

Mitch had gotten the gun about three weeks ago. Caleb swiped it from an older cousin and gave it to him. If his dad had ever tried to pull one of his stunts again. If he had ever raised a hand at his mother again... Mitch would have been ready.

But he never needed to use it. And now he never would.

Mitch held it in his hands, staring at it. He wondered how his life would have been different if he had the gun earlier. He raised it, imagining he was pointing it at his enraged dad just as he was about to hit his mom. He wouldn't have hesitated.

Mitch lowered his arm but kept staring at the pistol. If he would have had the gun earlier, he would also probably be in prison for murder.

But it didn't matter. He was safe. More importantly, his mom was safe. They could move on with their lives. He hated that they lost their house, but it was a small price to pay.

He stared at the gun in his hands.

This was all his dad's fault. Why had he been cursed with a monster for a father? Flashes of violence shot through his head. His father slapping his mother across the face. Dishes thrown across the room. Mitch would try to defend her, but his dad was big. His bicep burned at the memory of this father's grip. His ears rang as he felt his father's backhand again. His ankle seared at the memory of the cigarettes that had been burned out on him.

His hands were shaking, and he tightened his grip on the gun to help steady them.

He started rocking back and forth, the feelings of total helplessness and blind anger swirling together inside of him. The anger grew and morphed into a silent rage. Rage at all the horrible things he could never undo. Rage at his inability to protect his mother from all the terrible things his dad did.

A muffled thud outside snapped him out of it. He walked to the front of the shed and peered out the door. It was dark so it was hard to be sure, but it looked like there was a car in the driveway.

50

Sam pulled into Charlie's driveway, surprised to not see his truck. He had been trying to call him, but it had gone straight to voicemail every time.

He knew Charlie wouldn't react well to Sam's suggestion for him to go public. But it could be his only option. Once the warden was under media scrutiny, Charlie would be safer. The warden couldn't risk being implicated in another murder.

As Sam approached the front door, he noticed it wasn't completely shut. Sam's worry about Charlie's reaction immediately turned to worry that the warden may have already gotten to him. Sam slowly withdrew his gun from its shoulder holster and held it low, his finger on the trigger.

His heart was pounding in his ears as he pushed the front door open. The house was dark except for a dim glow coming from a room off of the entryway. Sam called out for Charlie, but there was no response.

Slowly, Sam walked through the house. When he reached the entryway to the room with the light, he peered around the door frame carefully. But the room was empty. He continued to walk room to room, checking them all. Never knowing what he would find. But, much to his relief, he found nothing.

Finally, assured that the house was empty, Sam loosened his grip on his gun. It was at that exact moment that his phone vibrated, causing him to jump and drop the gun to the floor. Gathering his composure, Sam picked up his gun while pulling his phone from his jacket pocket. He checked the Caller ID and let out a loud sigh of relief.

"Sam? It's me," Carla said on the other end of the line. "I just found something that you may want to know."

Sam walked through the house more casually now, turning on lights in each room as he went. The living room and bedroom seemed normal. Neat and tidy. No sign of Charlie, though.

"Is it about Rodriguez?" he asked.

"What? Oh. No," she replied. "Rodriguez died of smoke inhalation. There was no sign of any other injury."

Sam's heart sank a bit. He had been banking on some evidence to back up his theory.

"But that just means he was passed out when the fire started, not that he started it," Carla added.

"Yeah, but we can't prove that. I was really hoping..."

"Sam," she interrupted. "That's not why I'm calling. I found something else."

Carla told him how she had been doing research on Rodriguez and Reddington and how she had come across Joe's old yearbooks.

"There's one picture of Francine with a caption *Most Likely to Stay in Love Forever*," Carla said.

Sam smiled and nodded as he walked to the kitchen. "Yeah? Her and Joe, huh?"

He flipped on the light to the kitchen. This is clearly the room where Charlie had been last. An empty bottle of tequila lay on the table next to a glass. There was another bottle of liquor on the kitchen counter and what looked to be a broken glass on the floor.

"It wasn't Joe," Carla continued. "It was Charlie Paloma."

Sam froze. Charlie used to date Francine? Why had he not said anything?

"Isn't that the prison guard you spoke to?" Carla asked.

Sam didn't answer. His eyes were locked on something sitting on the kitchen counter.

"Sam? You there?" Carla asked through the phone.

But Sam was no longer listening. He stepped around the broken glass to get closer to the object on the kitchen counter.

It was a Red Diamond coffee can. The same kind of hard-to-get coffee can Sam had found at Joe's house. The one that had been filled with threatening notes.

51

Francine sighed at the sound of the doorbell. Ruth and Dale had gone to the football game and were going out afterward. Francine had been looking forward to having the night to herself and finally watching *The Bachelorette* with a glass of Zinfandel. It used to be the highlight of her week. Joe would always go to Mitch's football game, so it was one of the few times she could be alone. Sitting down to watch the show was a small step toward something normal again, and she had been looking forward to it all day.

Even though part of her had wanted to watch Mitch play, she was relieved when he had asked her not to come. She understood. It was probably hard on him—the first game without his father there. She'd go to the game next week. That would be the championship game anyway.

The doorbell rang again. It was probably someone looking for her sister. She could turn them away and return to her show fast enough. She paused the show and set her glass of wine down on the coffee table.

She looked through the peephole and sighed as she opened the door to a very drunk Charlie Paloma. He was leaning in the doorway and reeked of tequila and beer. And she couldn't help but notice the panic in his eyes.

"Did you hear the news?" he asked. "About Manny Rodriguez?"

Francine nodded. "The man who killed Joe?"

He nodded back.

"I fucked up," he slurred. He stepped forward and Francine found herself quickly moving aside. It was a knee-jerk reaction after years of getting out of the way as her drunk husband barreled in the front door. She regretted it immediately. What was he doing here? And what did he mean by "I fucked up."?

Maybe he just needed to be around someone who knew Joe. Joe didn't have a lot of friends. Maybe Charlie just didn't want to be alone. She reminded herself that he probably knew the killer, too.

"Did you know him? Rodriguez?"

Charlie nodded then stumbled to the side, catching himself on the edge of a chair. He looked intently at Francine. Enough to make her uncomfortable.

"They're probably coming for me next," he said. "I'm a dead man, Francine. But I had to see you first."

Francine was confused. What was he talking about? She was already trying to figure out a way to get him out of the house.

"You've had too much to drink," she said, leading him back toward the door. He stopped and spun around.

"I know you didn't love him," he slurred. The words hit her hard.

"I'm sorry?" was all she could muster.

"You don't have to feel guilty."

Francine was regretting letting him in the house. "He was my husband."

Charlie shrugged. "But you didn't love him. How could you? The way he treated you?"

Francine felt offended. Even though everything he was saying was true, it was not his place to say it.

"Charlie, I'm going to have to ask you to leave."

Charlie nodded, realizing he had gone too far. He shut his eyes as if it would force him to sober up.

"I'm sorry. That was out of line," he mumbled. "I'm just... I don't know what to do."

He fell into her, sobbing into her shoulder. "I blew it," he cried. "I messed everything up."

Francine was caught off guard and wasn't sure what to do. She patted his back gently.

"You're just drunk," she said. "You'll feel different tomorrow."

He pulled away.

"I may not be alive tomorrow," he said through his tears.

Then he stopped and tried to gain his composure. Francine felt relieved that the situation was calming down.

He smiled at her and nodded. "You always understood me," he said quietly.

"Charlie, you need to go now," Francine said firmly.

But Charlie didn't seem to hear her. He stared into her eyes and took a step toward her.

"I never stopped loving you," he said. Then he stepped toward her quickly, pushing her back against the wall and pressing against her.

"Stop it!" she yelled as she tried to push him away. But he had leaned his weight into her and she was pinned helplessly. He quickly pushed his lips on hers. He tasted like tequila and she turned her head to avoid his sloppy kisses. She fought against him with all her strength, trying to peel him off of her.

Then a voice yelled out, catching both of them off guard.

"Get away from my mom!"

They both turned toward the voice.

It was Mitch. And he had a gun.

52

Sam pushed the accelerator to the floor. No one was answering their phones. Not Francine. Not Mitch. Not even Charlie.

"How could I have been so stupid?" Sam thought to himself.

Charlie had been leading him along the entire time. He led him to Rodriguez, knowing there was enough bad blood between the ex-con and Joe Reddington to make him an obvious suspect. And when Sam had hesitated to make an arrest, Charlie tried to seal the deal by planting the threatening notes in Joe's garage.

What Charlie hadn't counted on was how far Warden Stivek was willing to go to keep his prison scandal buried. When Rodriguez wound up dead, Charlie must have shit his pants. It wouldn't take long for the warden to figure out Charlie was the leak. By using the scandal to throw Rodriguez under the bus, Charlie had wound up putting a target on his own back.

Sam remembered Charlie's phone messages earlier in the day. He had sounded panicked. That scared Sam. Panicked men do stupid things.

As Sam raced on to the street where Francine and Mitch

were staying, he slowed down to a crawl. As he neared the house, his heart sank. It was what he was afraid of. Charlie's truck was in their driveway.

53

Francine was frozen in shock. She saw a blind rage in Mitch's eyes that scared her. His mouth was twisted in a violent sneer. He was visibly shaking and had to use both hands to steady the gun in front of him.

Charlie raised his hands in surrender. "Mitch. Put the gun down."

"Shut up!" Mitch interrupted.

Francine tried to urge her son to put the gun down, but he didn't even seem to hear her voice.

"You were hurting her," Mitch growled. "I saw it."

"I'm fine, Mitch," Francine said. "He didn't hurt me."

Mitch looked at his mom.

"Why do you always let them get away with it?" he yelled.

"No one's getting away with anything," Charlie said calmly. "Let's not do anything rash."

Sam peeked in the front window and was shocked by what he saw. Mitch had a gun on Charlie and his mother? He crept along the shadows to the back of the house, trying to figure out a plan. He needed to quickly de-escalate the situation. Running into the house pointing a gun would just make things worse and the wrong people could get hurt. Hell, he could get hurt.

At the back of the house, he saw a sliding glass door was open.

"Good," Sam thought. "Less noise."

As he crept inside, he devised a plan. It certainly wasn't fool-proof, but it was his best bet. Taking a deep breath, he tucked his pistol back in the shoulder holster.

"Here goes nothing," he muttered to no one in particular.

54

Mitch was sweating bullets, the gun was still aimed at Charlie's head. When his mother tried to take a step toward him, he swung the gun toward her.

"You stay back, Mom," he said, then turned the gun back to Charlie. "We're not going to be victims anymore."

"There you are!" Sam's voice bellowed out of nowhere from behind them.

Mitch, Francine and Charlie all turned to see Sam walk casually into the room.

"I have been looking all over for you, buddy," Sam said loudly to Charlie.

He walked up next to a stunned Mitch, who was still half-pointing the gun at Charlie.

"Hey, Mitch. Hey, Francine," he said casually.

He looked at the gun Mitch was still gripping tightly and shook his head.

"You've got to be careful there; son," Sam said to Mitch. "You could shoot someone with one of those things."

He casually reached for the gun, hoping to catch Mitch off guard. But Mitch snapped out of shock. As they wrestled for the gun, Charlie pushed Francine to take cover behind a chair. Sam was finally able to yank the pistol away from the teen, but it slipped from his hands and fell to the ground with a loud clatter.

Francine ran to her son.

"Mitch, stop it!"

To keep the gun out of Mitch's reach until he could calm him down, Sam kicked it. Then watched helplessly as it slid across the room... and stopped directly at Charlies' feet.

"Shit," thought Sam.

The drunk guard stared down at the pistol. Sam froze, waiting to see what Charlie's next move would be.

Francine held her son back as he yelled at Sam for interfering. He told him that Charlie was attacking his mother and he was trying to protect her. Sam looked to Francine for confirmation, but she meekly shook her head no.

"It was just a misunderstanding," she said.

Sam nodded, not convinced, and asked Charlie if that were true.

Charlie laughed nervously. "Yeah, just a misunderstanding."

"Bullshit!" Mitch yelled.

But Sam wasn't paying attention to the teenager. His eyes were locked on Charlie. He noticed the way Charlie looked at Francine when he spoke. He could sense the bitterness in his voice. And he could feel the tension in the air. He knew he needed to keep Charlie occupied and move him away from the gun.

Sam could feel his own gun, stuck in its shoulder holster. There was no way he could get to it fast enough. Charlie would beat him to the draw for sure. His best bet was to distract him.

"I've been looking for you," Sam said to Charlie. "I need to get you someplace safe."

Charlie's face went white. "Why?"

Sam lied that he had gotten permission to put Charlie into protective custody until they could catch the men responsible for Rodriguez's death.

Charlie seemed to think about it for a second, then shook his head.

"I don't believe you," he said.

Sam laughed, trying to pretend he thought Charlie was joking.

"Why would I lie to you, buddy?" he asked.

Charlie shook his head. It was clear he was nervous and flustered. He looked down at the gun again.

"Come on, we've got to get out of here before they figure out where you are," Sam said.

But when he took a step forward, Charlie panicked. He reached down and picked up the gun, pointing it at Sam. Sam raised his hands in surrender.

None of this is going as I planned it, thought Sam.

"Stay back," Charlie said as his eyes darted back and forth between Sam and Francine.

"Charlie? What are you doing? It's me," Sam acted surprised.

"Throw your gun down," Charlie demanded.

Sam tried to play dumb about having a gun but then realized, with his hands in the air, the shoulder holster was in plain sight. He slowly pulled the gun out of the holster. Maybe he could make a quick move, flip his gun around and aim it at Charlie. Sam pulled the gun out and, following Charlie's orders, placed it on the ground and slid it carefully over to Charlie.

So much for Plan B. And C. And probably D.

Sam had to think of something to distract Charlie. Something that would throw him off.

"You didn't tell me you and Francine used to be a thing," he said casually.

Charlie froze.

"High school sweethearts, right?" Sam asked, not taking his eyes off of Charlie. "Why didn't you tell me?"

Charlie's face tightened. "That was a long time ago."

Sam shrugged. "That must've been a real kick in the gonads, having to work with Joe every day."

Charlie glared at Sam, angry that he had brought up Joe's name.

"Charlie," Francine said softly.

"You just... erased everything," Charlie snapped at her. "And then treated me like I didn't even exist."

"He wouldn't let me talk to you," Francine said.

"He treated you like shit," Charlie answered. "He even bragged about it."

Knowing he wasn't going to be able to get Charlie outside, Sam shifted gears and started to focus on disarming the situation.

"You wanted to save her," Sam interjected. "I get it. That's what I'd do for the woman I loved."

Charlie shook his head, his gun still pointing at Sam.

"I helped you," he said. "I told you about Rodriguez. I gave you information that could get me killed."

"You know what was weird?" Sam asked. "The way Joe kept all of those threatening notes. Why would he do that?"

Charlie struggled to answer and Sam took a half step toward him.

"But he didn't, did he?" Sam asked. "You wrote them, didn't you? You wrote them and planted them in the garage so I would find them."

"Why would I do that?" Charlie stammered.

"You put them in a coffee can," Sam went on. "Red Diamond, right?"

Charlie didn't say anything.

"Francine, y'all drink Red Diamond coffee?" Sam asked.

Francine was confused. "What? No."

"What's going on?" Mitch yelled. "What are you saying?"

Charlie was almost backed up against the wall, but Sam was still too far away to make any kind of move.

"Come on, Charlie," he said calmly. "Put down the gun. You're not a bad guy. You were trying to save the woman you love from a bad guy. That's heroic. Don't let that scumbag Rodriguez get credit for what you did."

The words seemed to strike a nerve with Charlie. He stood up straighter and the panic in his eyes slowly melted into a proud resolve.

"He was a bad man, Francine," Charlie said. "He was worse than you even know."

Confused, Francine began to cry.

"I did it for you," Charlie continued.

Francine nodded at Charlie, unable to speak. Mitch, who had been trying to absorb everything that was going on, finally spoke.

"You killed my dad?" he asked with a combination of anger and curiosity in his voice.

Charlie looked at the kid, trying to figure out exactly what to say. He finally just nodded. He turned his attention back to Francine. A single tear trailed down his cheek as he gently smiled at her. Then, with one swift motion, he turned the gun toward himself. Sam dove at him just as the shot echoed through the house.

55

Sam stepped out of the hospital room and let out a heavy sigh. Charlie had been in the hospital for a week now. Luckily, Sam had tackled him just as he pulled the trigger and Charlie had wound up only clipping an ear. He'd lost a lot of blood, as well as the hearing in his right ear, but he was recovering well.

After Charlie's arrest, Nancy Hellard decided to start digging on her own. After interviewing several guards and inmates, she had uncovered enough information for a feature story on the corruption at the prison, including Maria Rodriguez's sexual assault and suicide cover-up. The story was quickly picked up by national news outlets, and the scandal had forced the resignation of Warden Stivek. With the case now under a proper police investigation, heads were starting to roll. Chief Kaster was on a paid leave of absence, pending an investigation into abuse of power related to the prison scandal.

As soon as Charlie was able to speak, he issued a full confession to the murder of Joe Reddington and to setting fire to his house.

On the night of the murder, Charlie had gone over to Joe's

house to confront him about his treatment of Francine. But Joe had laughed him off as usual. This time, Charlie had had enough. He followed Joe up to his bedroom and, grabbing one of Joe's old baseball trophies off the dresser, hit him over the head. The blow had hit Joe at just the right angle and velocity to be lethal. Panicked at first, Charlie took a page from the stories he had heard from some of the inmates. He placed Joe in bed and staged the house fire, thinking it would be ruled an accident. It had all gone better than he could have hoped.

He was shocked when Sam showed up at the prison and told him they were investigating Joe's death as a murder. But he knew about the Rodriguez situation and decided to use it to his favor. He had hoped circumstantial evidence would be enough to frame the ex-con. Then, when Sam had confided that he wasn't sure about his guilt, Charlie decided to give him a push by writing the notes and planting them in Joe's garage. His only mistake was using a coffee can that could be linked to him.

But Charlie didn't have anything to do with Rodriguez's death. And when he heard about it, he knew right away the warden was tying up loose ends. He panicked and made a hasty decision to get out of town. But he needed to see Francine one last time.

What he hadn't counted on was Sam's tenacity. After meeting with the detective at the prison, he had asked around and had been told that Sam Lawson was a lazy cop who always looked for the easy way out. Charlie had thought he was home free.

But Sam surprised everyone, especially himself. He had forgotten how good it felt to work a case. To solve it. And, so what if the system spit a lot of the bad guys back? Two steps forward and one step back is still one step forward. He didn't need to obsess on it like he used to. But giving a damn isn't an all or nothing proposition. He could "care in moderation."

Now it was time to stop talking about getting his life in order and actually start doing it. He knew it wouldn't be easy. Old habits die hard. But he was determined. It didn't hurt that he had Carla's support. She believed in him, and he wasn't going to let her down.

He also wasn't going to let his son down, whether he liked it or not. He had scheduled some vacation time and had booked a flight to California. His son had reluctantly agreed to meet him for coffee. And that was a good start. Even if it ended right there, he would know he tried.

"How's he doing?" a woman's voice asked.

Sam looked up as Carla approached him. She seemed to get more beautiful to him every day. She smiled at him, as if she could read his mind, and gave him a peck on the cheek.

Sam caught Carla up on Charlie's status. He'd be well enough to face arraignment soon, and he seemed to be at peace with it. Knowing he had given Francine and Mitch a fresh start really did seem to be enough for him.

Sam looked up at the television monitor, which was broadcasting a 24-hour news channel. Nancy Hellard stood in front of the prison, and Sam read the closed captioning on the screen as the reporter spoke:

"Today, Gary Stivek, former warden of Quinton State Penitentiary, was arrested in connection with the murder of Manuel Rodriguez. Mr. Stivek had recently stepped down as warden due to his role in the ongoing guard rape scandal..."

Sam smiled. He was glad Rodriguez finally got justice, even if it was after he died.

Carla slipped her arm into his and the two headed toward the exit.

"You sure you don't want to come with me to California?" he asked.

"I think you need to do this trip on your own," she replied. "But I'll be here when you get back."

He grinned. "That's something I'll definitely be looking forward to."

His grin widened into a smile. He may not have all the answers. Hell, he hardly had any of them. But he knew he was ready to handle whatever came his way. And that's more than he'd felt in a very long time.

THANK YOU FOR READING
COMBUSTIBLE!
If you enjoyed it, be sure to leave a review wherever you bought
your copy.

GET A FREE COPY OF *BOUND BY MURDER*
Go back to Sam Lawson's first murder case in this fun and
riveting e-novella. Get your free copy at
davidkwilsonauthor.com

ENJOY MORE OF THE
SAM LAWSON MYSTERY SERIES:
COMBUSTIBLE
DARK HARBOR
BENEATH THE SURFACE
DEADLY REPUTATION
DEATH ON LOCATION

ALSO BY DAVID K. WILSON:
RED DIRT BLUES
"Wildly entertaining and absurdly funny!" Nothing goes as
planned when a cold-blooded thief is pulled into the quirky
and colorful lives of a motley crew of rednecks.

Learn more at davidkwilsonauthor.com

Acknowledgments

It goes without saying that this book never could have happened without the help and support of so many.

First off, thanks to Ashley Previte for her ruthless editing. A huge thanks also goes to my first readers, Cathie Cotten, Sandy Gottehrer, Glory-Anne Jones, Cathie Neumiller, James Hewitson and Yvonne Pelletier. Their input was invaluable and I am so grateful for their help. Likewise, thanks to Tim Nerney, who lent his firefighting expertise to keep me honest, and Mike Rodgers, who graciously lent his design talent to help me with my book cover and website.

I also have to give a special thanks to Jennifer Jaynes, whose advice, friendship and encouragement have been invaluable.

Then there are my kids: Alayna, Colin and Mallory. They are my reason. Simple as that.

Finally, I must thank my parents Jim and Barbara (I call them Mom and Dad, but we have a special relationship like that) for always believing in me and encouraging me to pursue my passions. There are no finer role models - and friends - in the world.

Cover design by Caroline Johnson

Cover images @ Adobestock

ABOUT THE AUTHOR

David K. Wilson grew up in East Texas, surrounded by enough colorful characters to fill the pages of hundreds of books. He has been an advertising copywriter and creative director, and is probably responsible for some of the junk mail you've received. He is also a seasoned ghostwriter and screenwriter. He currently lives in upstate New York, where he still complains about winter every single year. COMBUSTIBLE is his debut novel.

Sign up to receive updates on David's next novel at
davidkwilsonauthor.com

Follow David on social media:

f facebook.com/davidkwilsonauthor

◎ instagram.com/davidkwilsonauthor

g goodreads.com/davidkwilson

Made in United States
North Haven, CT
23 January 2023

31494259R00129